THE
FIRST
SECRET

MAYA DANIELS

Vinci Books

vinci-books.com

Published by Vinci Books Ltd in 2026

1

Copyright © Maya Daniels 2019

The author has asserted their moral right to be identified as the author of this work in accordance with the Copyright, Designs and Patents Act 1988. This work is a work of fiction. Names, characters, places and incidents are the product of the author's imagination or are used fictitiously. Any resemblance to actual persons, living or dead, places and incidents is entirely coincidental.
All rights reserved. No part of this publication may be copied, reproduced, distributed, stored in any retrieval system, or transmitted in any form or by any means, including photocopying, recording, or other electronic or mechanical methods, nor used as a source for any form of machine learning including AI datasets, without the prior written permission of the publisher.
The publisher and the author have made every effort to obtain permissions for any third party material used in this book and to comply with copyright law. Any queries in this respect should be brought to the attention of the publisher and any omissions will be corrected in future editions.
A CIP catalogue record for this book is available from the British Library.
Paperback ISBN: 9781036705909
The EU GPSR authorised representative is Logos Europe, 9 rue Nicolas Poussion, 17000 La Rochelle, France contact@logoseurope.eu

By Maya Daniels

Hidden Portals Trilogy
Venus Trap
The First Secret

Chronicles of Forbidden Witchery
Resting Witch Face
Pitch a Witch
Witch Please
Payback is a Witch

The Necronomicon Guardian
The Magician
The High Priestess

The Broken Halos Series
The Devil is in the Details
Speak of the Devil
Encounter with the Devil
The Devil in Disguise
To Look the Devil in the Eye
Better The Devil You Know
Give a Devil His Due

The Last Note Series
Sound

Sonata

Daywalker Series
Investigated
Infiltrated
Instigated
Initiated
Infuriated
Ignited

Infernal Regions for the Unprepared
Black Hand
Lower World
Everlasting Fire
Place of Torment
Hellfire To Come

The Courtless Fae Series
Secret Origins

New Blood Rising
Rebirth - Risorgimento
Overthrown - Rovesciamento
Recognition - Riconoscimento

The Gatekeepers Legacy
Legacy of Water
Legacy of Fire
Legacy of Spirit

Honor Among Thieves

Stolen Magic

Stolen Oath

By Maya Daniels

The Cursed Kingdom

Prologue

Sitting cross-legged in the middle of the large room dedicated to her goddess, clutching the Fae arrow in her trembling hands, Iris stared at nothing. The last remnants of the portal she'd opened for Artemis and Raphael were fading. Little flashes of sparks reminded her of her situation. Iris kept the portal open for a long time, unsure if she was hallucinating. Without thought her thumb stroked the arrow. Zaps of magic shot up her arm numbing it all the way to the shoulder. Her magic spread around the room like a curious sentient entity in the form of tendrils of dark purple smoke.

Iris didn't register the candles floating in midair all around her, their flames flaring in bursts as the markings on the arrow glowed with a blueish spark. Part of her brain knew that she should release it and prepare to pull the stubborn vampire out of the Fae realm, yet, she sat there.

'Never make a deal with the devil on an empty stomach' her mother used to say, but Iris had never understood the meaning of it until a week ago. Curiosity had always got her into trouble. She'd never learned the lesson to stay out of things that didn't concern her, and surviving her current peculiar predicament seemed unlikely.

At first, that damn vampire had intrigued her with his beauty. Not handsome, that would've meant he possessed some imperfection that made him at least a little human. Iris didn't see any harm in letting him watch her ritual. In her defense, no sane woman would've said no to Raphael hanging around. So, stupidly, she'd helped him when he brought Artemis to her, unconscious and hardly breathing. Iris realized that the vampire would never look at any other woman but the one he cradling to his chest like the most precious thing in the world. Being honest with herself, she knew that she only tried to like Raphael because she couldn't get a certain man out of her head. Well a Fae, not a man, but that made no difference to her stupid heart.

A prickling sensation, like fire ants crawling all over her body, jolted her out of her internal musings. She couldn't remember the last time she'd been this jumpy but having crazy immortals around, itching for a fight, would do that to a person. Another wave hit her as she tried to push herself up off the floor. Stumbling and nearly falling on her face, Iris hurried, holding the hem of her dress in both hands but not letting go of the arrow. She'd promised Artemis that she would be ready if they needed her, and she'd be damned if she didn't keep her word. The arrow would be glued to her until everything settled.

The prickling intensified as she jerked the heavy door open and ran down the hall. Only someone trying to break through one of her protections could cause this internal burning. She'd placed one around the store after the fiasco with the vampire king. Otherwise, there was only one thing she protected here, and no one but her knew about that.

The First Secret

With her heart in her throat, she ran through the curtain separating the store from the rooms behind it, and almost tripped over her feet in the process.

"Damn curtains and stupid hallways..." she muttered while flailing her arms to detangle herself from the black fabric. Bursting into the store she almost toppled a couple of statues to the floor.

The few LAD candles with their fake flames gave off only enough light to make out objects. Still, not wanting to break anything, she tiptoed carefully towards the large front windows. The streetlight provided enough yellowish hue that even before reaching the glass Iris could tell no one lurked there. The feeling of her insides burning increased, and her eyebrows scrunched up in confusion and pain when nothing but an occasional vehicle passed by.

The arrow in her hand hummed proving that either Artemis, or Raphael, was in trouble, yet the urge to find out who was trying to get through her protection grew stronger. Reaching for the doorknob in hopes of finding answers outside the store, she jumped when something topped over in the hallway and a voice muttered.

Panic gripped her like an iron fist, Iris Forgot about vamps, Fae and their realm. Her feet barely touched the ground as she ran to the back rooms. At the end of the hallway, in front of an empty wall, a figure hunched over picking up a fallen painting.

"Danny?" Gasping for air, Iris bent over. Placing her hands on her knees, she almost nicked herself with the arrow.

With a high-pitched shriek, the blond woman dropped on her ass, her eyes as wide as dinner plates as she clutched her chest with both hands.

"Oh my god, Iris! You scared the crap out of me!"

"Your god is not here, Danny, and I'll scare even more crap out of you if you don't tell me what you are doing here." Still gasping, Iris glared at the other woman.

"I work here." Danny lifted her eyebrows clearly wondering if her boss had lost her mind. "Remember?"

"I didn't mean in the store, smartass. I meant here, in the hallway."

"Oh…" Danny fidgeted with her hands before slowly lifting herself up without looking at Iris. "I had an urge to check this area." Her face turned red, and she stumbled over her words. "You always talk about intuition, and just knowing stuff, and I had this thing." She gazed shyly at Iris. "Like a knowing… that I needed to come here. But then I bumped the painting, and then you scared the crap out of me… To be honest, I thought Raphael was here." Danny's face turned beet red, as she looked at anything but Iris.

"Go home, Danny." Iris pressed a hand over her forehead. "Forget about the vampire, he is nothing but trouble. Take a few days off, and I'll see you next week. I need some time to sort things out."

"Am I getting fired?" Danny's chin trembled.

"Why on earth would you think that? No, I just think after everything, we could both use a break."

"That's true." With a relieved sigh, Danny smiled tightly, and without another word walked towards the store front.

Iris stood there, heart thundering, thanking whoever watched over her for hiding her panic at Danny's intuition calling her to this very spot. As soon as the blonde hair disappeared through the curtain, Iris turned and traced an invisible line on the wall from top to bottom with her hand. Not touching it, her fingers hovered an inch or so from the plaster. The purple glow emitted from her palm reflected on the wall, lighting it up and revealing the door that no one else but her could detect. It troubled her that Danny would stop at this very spot. Swallowing the nervousness, Iris pushed the door open and stepped inside.

It was a small room, a 'just in case' hideaway. Nothing in it apart from a bed, a chair and a dresser with a few medical supplies, some clothing, and blankets. Everything looked identical to how she'd left it, including the sleeping Fae who had not woken since the day he'd been pulled into this realm alongside Artemis via a portal during one of her rituals. The same Fae who had haunted her thoughts ever since. He resembled a sculpture rather than a living being. His long silky black hair spread out around his unusually perfect face and his pointy ears peeked out of it. Unable to help herself, Iris reached out and traced his angular jaw and full lips with her fingers. She'd been willing him to wake up for over a week, but nothing helped. As she'd done every day since he'd arrived, she prepared to send her magic inside him, to make sure he still lived.

A terrified scream echoed around the store and hallway. Iris's head snapped toward the closed door and the blood drained from her face. Danny's voice echoed in a painful scream a moment before sounds of breaking glass and the stock being smashed and turned over. Her mind stuttered trying to think of what to do. Terror paralyzed her when a voice she recognized echoed out from the store.

"Witch! You better show yourself, or your little friend here will give more than just a little blood," Claude called out.

"Shit! Crappity crap...damn it!" Iris muttered through clenched teeth knowing she had nowhere to run. More crashing came from the shop before energy stirred in the hallway as Claude passed the curtain.

"Witch, witch, witch..." He sang the word in some mocking song as he banged his fist on the walls. "Come out, come out, witch."

Taking a deep breath, Iris squared her shoulders. Claude might possess more physical strength, he'd almost killed her once, but she wasn't a helpless little puppy. She had teeth, and she would bite if cornered. And she was cornered, if she wanted to protect the unconscious Fae from the vampire. Steeling herself, she gripped the arrow tighter in her fist and stepped towards the door. Her heart froze, and her feet gave out when a thick arm wrapped around her waist and another grabbed her mouth cutting off her automatic scream. A second later, the scent of rainforest and freshly cut grass filled her nostrils making her sag in the hold of the man behind her.

"Don't make a sound, witch. We need to run," Fern whispered from behind her, his deep musical voice making her shiver. "We need to run, now!"

Chapter One

"Oh, hell no!" With her eyebrows pulled down, and her hands on her hips, Iris glared at Raphael and Artemis. "I'm not going anywhere with that lying weirdo, and there is nothing you can say to convince me otherwise!" Stomping her foot for emphasis, and angrily pointing a finger at Ivy, she lifted her chin.

"Witch, you're pushing your luck right now, and patience is not one of my strong suits," Raphael growled through clenched teeth.

"It's not?" Iris gasped pressing her hands on her chest. "I never would've guessed!" She did everything she could to maintain her innocent expression although Artemis snickering didn't help.

"You are encouraging her obnoxious behavior." Raphael turned his disapproving glare on his mate. Artemis raised one eyebrow. That's all it took for the stubborn vampire to turn to mush and give her a soft smile.

"You have no right in this realm, or the next, to call

anyone obnoxious, especially after what I witnessed!" Not deterred, Iris continued by waving a finger in the vampire's face.

His gaze narrowed. Lightning fast, he snatched her finger in his large hand. Iris didn't expect it, and pure instinct made her magic light up like a Christmas tree in her chest. It burst out of her and knocked him a few feet in the air before he dropped into a cat-like crouch. Eyes glowing and fangs bared, Raphael appeared almost feral. Iris lifted both hands to protect herself in case he pounced. Artemis moved in front of her to calm Raphael down, but Ivy stood to the side watching everything unfold with a huge smile on her face. It pissed Iris off even more.

"Raphael." Even Iris shivered at Artemis's low sultry tone. "She is scared and worried. Her life was in danger because of us, because of me, and we were not there to protect her as we promised. Lashing out at you is her way of dealing with it."

"I'm neither scared, not worried just so we are clear," Iris chirped from behind Artemis making Ivy chuckle.

"You're not helping." Looking over her shoulder, Artemis looked pointedly at Ivy.

"Okay, fine!" Huffing, Iris crossed her arms over her chest. "Sorry boss man, I didn't mean to zap you. In my defense, you startled me. And ever since I stepped foot here, my magic has been flaring up. I'm trying my best to keep it under control." She shrugged, but no one was fooled at her nonchalance. Her expressive green eyes betrayed the fear lurking inside.

They were standing outside the palace where Artemis had taken Iris to show her the extent of the deterioration of the realm. The Dreamweaver, Ivy, was adamant that Iris

The First Secret

was of the ancient line needed to heal the realm of the Fae. Iris wanted to argue about that little detail, she figured it'd be useless. Every time she tried to explain that she didn't understand where her magic came from, Ivy cut her mid-sentence, saying that time would prove it.

The hairs on the back of Iris's neck prickled and she scanned the area without being obvious about it. Someone was watching her, and anxiety swirled in her stomach.

"You are a walking disaster, witch." Raphael, ignorant of her unease, continued. "Maybe it would be smarter to send you back to the human realm." Blood drained from Iris's face. "I'm worried the Fae might kill you if one of us is not around you." Placing his hands on his hips, he looked at her solemnly as if he'd stated the most reasonable solution to her problems.

"No..." her voice was barely above a whisper as she forced that one word through numb lips.

"You don't know what you are talking about, bloodsucker!" Ivy's face darkened, dimming the golden glow around her. "Are you trying to doom us all by getting her killed?"

"She can't control her magic! Any of the warriors would skin her alive if she did that to them! She doesn't think, she reacts!"

"Now listen to me, and listen very good, you bullheaded man!" Ivy snarled, not caring that Artemis gave her a side-eye while Raphael glared.

Iris missed the rest of the exchange as Artemis threaded her arm through hers and pulled her towards the large open double doors of the palace. Iris let Artemis lead her. Her mind still spun from the creepy sensation of being watched, plus Raphael's comment about sending her back to where Claude waited. The Fae milling around the front courtyard stopped and bowed their heads in respect, placing their fists over their heart as they had done ever since Artemis killed Lazarus. Iris ignored them.

"I don't want to go inside the palace," she blurted. Artemis stopped in her tracks and raised her eyebrows.

"Don't ask for a reason right now, I can't give you one. I just feel like I'll never come out alive if I walk through those doors." Iris was grateful that Artemis didn't dismiss her like Raphael would've done.

Artemis might be a ruthless bitch, feared by Fae and vampires alike, but the other woman never did anything simply for the sake of hurting or killing someone. Iris felt a kinship connecting them, and at the moment her only hope to stay alive lay in Artemis's hands.

"Talk to me, Iris." Looking at her intently, Artemis grabbed her shoulders. "You know you can tell me anything. Who has scared you so much under my roof?"

"No one, I swear." Shaking her head in frustration, Iris sighed deeply. "I can't explain it… There is someone…no, there is something inside watching me. I can feel it every time I'm inside the palace, and I also felt it when we were standing outside."

"I'm not dismissing your worries, my friend. But, I'm not sure if you have noticed, my kind kinda likes you." With her lips curling up in a smile, Artemis tilted her chin indicating the Fae walking around them. "We like pretty things," she winked at Iris, "and you are a beautiful woman. Plus, not many of them have seen the human realm. To us, you are exotic, unusual. If you need to let off some steam, I'm sure many will be more than happy to take on the task. From what I know, humans don't have a problem with casual sex."

"Oh my god, no!" Iris looked at her friend, horrified. "Some humans don't have a problem with it, but most do. I'm one of those. The ones that mind." Waving her hand as if chasing a fly, Iris sighed again. "This is different from being checked out. I'm sure I look like a circus monkey to them and that's why they're staring. I mean, look at them!" Moving her arm in an arc, she indicated all the drool-worthy specimens around her. "They are so perfect, they don't look real... or normal. Me? I'm just, I donno... human?" Chuckling humorlessly, she covered her face with her hands. "I sound pathetic and like a scared little mouse. It's so not me; I have no idea why I'm acting like this."

Artemis's jaw clenched. "Raphael!" called to her mate so loudly that Iris jumped a little.

"What's wrong?" Before the echo of Artemis's voice faded Raphael was next to them fangs gleaming and eyes glowing. Iris stared with her eyebrows up to her hairline, as confused at Artemis's reaction as Raphael seemed.

"Search the palace." Not taking her gaze off Iris, Artemis pursed her lips and released a soft whistle that had dozens of warriors almost materialize around them with hands on their weapons. "Search with all your senses, not only your sight. We have an uninvited guest that I want to personally welcome to our realm. I want to see whoever it is alive and on their knees in front of me by tonight."

Raphael barked additional orders. Ivy rushed to Iris's side saying things like 'You should've told me straight away if you felt someone was here, silly child,' but Iris couldn't stop staring at Artemis with her jaw dropped to her chest.

Artemis believed her. Not only did she believe her, but she took being cautious to a whole new level by dispatching dozens of deadly men and women to spread like a wave through the enormous building. Within seconds they were all gone, including Raphael, leaving the three women alone in the courtyard.

"Iris?" Tentatively, as if talking to a wounded animal and not wanting to spook it, Artemis reached for her. "Talk to me. Do you feel something that makes you look like that?"

"What? Oh, no!" Shaking her head to clear it, Iris grabbed both of Artemis's hands in hers. "Thank you!" Artemis's face softened. "Thank you for believing me."

"Your safety is not something I'm willing to leave to chance. If there is anyone or anything in the palace that wishes you ill, we will know in no time. Let us sit for a while," Artemis said and walked towards one of the handfuls of small patches around the palace that still had green grass sprinkled with white flowers. "Raphael will fetch us when it's safe, and I'm not letting you out of my sight until I'm certain."

"I wish we knew if Fern is safe, too." Guilt stabbed Iris's chest. It'd been three days, and still no sign of him. She plopped ungracefully next to Artemis with a heavy sigh, followed by Ivy.

"He'll be here sooner than you think," Ivy told them with a smile. Iris and Artemis both glared at her.

"You knew he was safe, and you didn't think to mention it?" Without thought, Iris touched her thumb to the rest of her fingers in rapid motion. The air around the three of them thickened with magic.

"Calm down, Iris." Lifting both hands in surrender Ivy's smile dropped. "I never said he was safe, just that he will be here before you know it. That's all I'm sure of."

The movement of her fingers stopped as Iris realized the sensation in her chest meant Ivy told the truth. Not wanting to sound crazier than she already did, Iris nodded jerkily. Deep down, she prayed that the Fae woman's intuition was right, and Fern would be back soon. They trusted her with his safety, and she'd almost got them both killed. The thought sat heavy in her heart, but there was nothing she could do but wait and hope he returned alive.

Chapter Two

"Keep your eyes closed and clear your mind." Ivy's voice ground on Iris's nerves. "You can't connect to anything if your mind is full of nonsense."

"I'm trying!" Iris snapped through clenched teeth, her nostrils flaring. "It's not like I want to think of something else." Her own defensiveness pissed her off.

"That's the problem. You are trying." Still calm, Ivy kept talking, and Iris wanted to zap her so bad. She yelped when a spark burst from her fingertips. Artemis reclining on her elbows, watching them. She covered her chuckle with a cough.

"What am I looking for exactly?" Opening one eye, Iris scowled at Ivy. "If I know what it is, I might find it sooner."

"When you sense it, you'll know," came the simple, irritating answer.

"Okay, Dali Lama!" Muttering under her breath, Iris closed her eyes and concentrated on breathing evenly again. "You'll know when you sense it," she mimicked Ivy's voice, and Artemis laughed. Ivy huffed under her breath; frustra-

The First Secret

tion radiated from the other woman, and a smile stretched Iris's lips.

"Both of you act like younglings." Ivy huffed, and the other two snickered until Ivy joined them. "I just know that you will feel your ancestors call when you need it most. Since you feel like you are in danger, I figured it was worth a try while we wait."

"And when I sense whatever it is, then what?"

"I don't know!" Throwing both arms up in frustration Ivy pressed her lips together in displeasure. "I'm sure you'll have guidance. It's a knowing."

Iris wanted to give Ivy an exasperated look, but a moving shadow from the corner of her eye had alarms flared inside her. On instinct, she threw her hands in the air, palms up, symbols lit up the center of them in a split second. Scorching heat burst out of her hands, creating a purple dome-like barrier around all three of them. Her arms burned, but she couldn't pull them down. Artemis jumped, shifting in her dragonfly form. Ivy's glow intensified, almost blinding Iris until she blinked and looked away from her. Panic clawed her chest and throat as her gaze landed on the shadow that had triggered her.

Grotesque, with eyes as white as snow on the smoky gray face, the shadow resembled some sort of animal. The narrow head had a snout-like muzzle, and long pointy ears stretched up six inches on top of its head. The eyes had no pupils or irises, just a white glow, but Iris could still tell it stared right at her. The body kept flicking through shapes, one second resembling a human with a torso, arms, and legs, and the next an animal with a flicking tail. It studied her as she examined it. Cold sweat trickled down Iris's spine.

Artemis moved like lightning, reaching through the

purple barrier and trying to grab hold of the shadow. When her hand passed through its smoke-like body, they both hissed and jerked back.

The shadow bared needle-like rows of teeth, and its hiss echoed like distant buzzing bees. Artemis hissed and then growled, cradling her arm to her chest. Her skin looked red and raw, and steam rose from it in the warm air as if it had been frozen. The shadow writhed, throwing itself at Iris's dome, then bouncing off before doing it all over again.

"What the hell is that thing?" Finally finding her voice, Iris still didn't look away from the shadow.

"I've never seen anything like it," Artemis growled, her violet eyes glowed menacingly at the shadow and her wings fluttering behind her in angry agitation.

Iris glanced at her friend before concentrating on the shadow again. "Just so we are clear, I would've totally freaked out if you were looking at me like you're looking at it right now." Nodding as if to back up her words she kept blabbing. "I don't think this thing has a brain. If I were it, I would've tucked my tail between my legs and ran. That's how scary you are."

"I think she loses the connection between her brain and mouth when scared," Ivy told Artemis nonchalantly with a small frown between her eyebrows.

"I can hear you." Iris glared at Ivy. "I just didn't want Artemis to think she's losing her touch at badassery or that she doesn't look as scary as any psycho bitch." Glancing at Artemis, Iris gave her a sharp nod. "You still have it! Don't let glow stick over there, poop on your parade. Even the shadow thing is scared. Look at it."

"I think you are right." Artemis nodded slowly at Ivy.

"Oh, my god! I'm trying to help!" Rolling her eyes, Iris tried to drop her arms again with no luck. The burning

The First Secret

sensation was getting worse, and she kept talking nonsense to stop herself screaming.

She hated that ever since she'd met Raphael and Artemis, it seemed like she needed saving from everything. "It's the worst feeling ever to try and do something, only to feel like a failure if you don't get the results you want. I didn't want you to feel like you failed. Sorry for trying to make you feel better." Lifting her chin, she turned away from both women. Right timing too since tears stung her eyes then streamed down her cheeks. She couldn't even wipe them off.

"Something is wrong." Clothing rustled as Artemis moved, and Iris's heart lodged in her throat. "Iris look at me." Grabbing both shoulders, she turned her towards them. "Ivy, she's seconds from passing out!" Urgency rang clear in Artemis's voice, and Ivy's glow intensified when she came closer.

"The protection is draining her. We must cut the connection. You think you can get her inside before that thing gets her?" Ivy sounded as if she was underwater.

Iris felt someone, probably Artemis, yanking on her arms, but they didn't move away from the shimmery purple mist. Voices raised, her body was pulled left and right like a doll, but all she could do was breathe and grind her teeth. The shadow hit the dome every few seconds, and each impact spiked like a nail to her brain. The pain was too much, and Iris wasn't sure that she wanted to stay alive stuck in the prison of her own body.

"It's too much. Too much!" Iris babbled to herself.

Blurry, through the tears flowing down her cheeks, Iris watched Ivy's glow brighten, and a determined expression settled on her pretty face. With lips pressed in a thin line, and eyes glowing more luminous than the sun, she reached both hands through the purple dome when the shadow threw itself at it again. When her hands went through its body, her glow blinked out a second after the shadow burst into dust particles. The instant the shadow vanished, the purple mist disappeared releasing its hold on Iris. Both, Ivy and Iris crumpled to the ground. Artemis screamed Raphael's name, and a roar echoed from the palace that froze Ivy's slowing heart before darkness took her

Chapter Three

Fern stumbled through the portal dropping to his hands and knees as soon as his entire body passed the shimmering barrier. Head hanging, he panted, trying to catch his breath after the chase he'd given the vampires around the forest. As much as he hated to admit it, even to himself, he was grateful for all the times Artemis forced him to train with her. Without that, he wouldn't have stayed one step ahead of the bloodsuckers. He would've been dead long ago if their king had gotten his hands on him.

"Fern?" a guard called out as he rushed inside the portal room. He only stopped when Fern could see the tips of his leather boots under his nose. "Is that you?"

Lifting his head with a groan, Fern turned and dropped on his ass, wincing when his body protested at the movement. Looking up, he tried to smile but failed miserably judging by the look on the other man's face.

"Darion, nice to see you too." With another groan, he lay fully on the cold floor and stared at the high ceiling.

"Excuse me for a blink until I catch my breath, my friend. Just make sure no one sees me like this."

Darion's citrine eyes flashed, betraying his alarm, but he nodded sharply before returning to the doors and standing in the threshold with his arms crossed over his chest. Fern knew he looked horrible and was grateful for the lack of questioning. His gratitude didn't last long.

Darion spoke over his shoulder, "You look like shit." The midnight hair falling down his broad back swayed as he turned to watch the hallway again. "What happened to you?"

"The ladies couldn't get enough of me." Fern tried for humor. "I barely escaped their grabby hands with my life." The attempt at chuckling failed as well, so he gave up and concentrated on trying to slow his breathing.

Darion hmphed under his breath. "I should fetch Artemis—"

"No!" Jerking his body up, Fern glared at the other man.

"You look one blink away from dying. You want Artemis to have my head if I don't tell her you are here? Did they take your brain in the human realm?"

"I'll tell her myself. And thank you, it's good to see you, too." Grinding his teeth, Fern lifted himself off the floor and swayed Darion rushed to his side and grabbed his arm.

"Maybe it'd be better if she came here. I'm not sure you can make it to the courtyard." Pulling Fern's arm over his shoulder, Darion led him slowly out of the portal room. "She's there with Ivy and that pretty human." A smile stretched his lips, mischief radiating from him. Fern wanted to punch him.

"The witch is okay?" His heart thumped at hearing that Iris was here safe, but he looked evenly at Darion as if he couldn't care less about her.

The First Secret

"She is more than okay." Darion wiggled his eyebrows. Fern clenched his fists. "She's been walking around the palace in those dresses making us follow behind her like lost pups. I have a bet going that I will get to her first. If only Artemis and Raphael leave her alone for a moment."

"Bet with whom?" Fern put as much curiosity as he could in his words while trying hard not to strangle his friend.

"Aaron. He thinks he has better odds because he is on guard at the front doors and sees her more often. He doesn't know she checks the portals every hour or so." Darion kept talking excitedly, and Fern's mind screeched to a halt.

Iris checked the portal room nonstop. Was she worried about him? Was it because she liked him, or did she feel responsible for him? And he really wanted to punch himself for even caring what she thought or wanted. She was a human, one with magic who meddled in things they couldn't control. They were to blame for this whole mess and the Fae realm dying. He should hate her, but he couldn't. It must be because she kept him alive, he decided.

"Maybe she is trying to escape back to her realm," he told Darion, and the other man frowned.

"Escape?" Snorting, he shook his head before another smile lit up his face. Fern ground his teeth loud enough to be heard. "Why would she try to escape? She is not a prisoner here. Artemis treats her like a close friend." Darion blinked. "I never thought she had friends...or even wanted one."

"And what am I?" Fern asked dryly.

"Her punching bag?" Darion snickered, earning another glare.

Fern kept his mouth shut because they'd entered the more populated areas. The other Fae stole glances at his ripped clothing, matted hair and grime covered skin, but he couldn't care less. When they reached the stairway that led to the front doors, Fern stopped dead in his tracks and jerked Darion back when the other man kept going. All his senses went on full alert as warriors appeared and disappeared through hallways and doors. They paid no attention to anyone around them, intent on their task.

"What's going on?" he said, not looking at Darion as he tracked the movements of the other Fae.

"Oh, that. We might have an unwanted visitor in the palace. The human sensed it. They'll find whoever it is in no time." Shrugging without a care in the world, Darion tried to keep walking but stumbled back when Fern grabbed his arm.

"What kind of unwanted visitor?" Ice piled up in the pit of his stomach.

"How would I know?" Looking at Fern like he'd lost his mind, Darion lifted both arms in frustration. "I'm stuck on guard duty in the portal room."

Fern's heart beat at an alarming rate again, and he snarled at his friend. "You're not guarding anything at the moment you idiot!" grabbing Darion's shoulder, he propelled him back toward where they'd come from. "Run!"

Darion paled and bolted back towards the portals. Fern grabbed the railing hoping to get himself down the stairs without falling and breaking his neck. He only managed two steps down when the air around him thickened with magic making it almost impossible to move.

"Iris..." He recognized the witch's magic. She'd fed it to his body for days to keep him alive. Fern felt almost connected to Iris through her magic, and he wasn't sure he liked that idea. She was a human, and not to be trusted at all.

Forcing his body to move, inch by a slow inch, he put as much force as he could but didn't make much progress. The other fae seemed just as affected, looking around in confusion, searching for the source of the magic. Surprisingly, no one appeared alarmed or uneasy instead they seemed curious, almost bored. The unusual reaction for a warrior race had his heart racing. Something was very wrong, and he couldn't do anything about it thanks to the damn witch.

Just as he thought he would go insane from being trapped and helpless, a pop echoed through the building. He almost went ass over head down the stairs when the thick magic vanished. Mouth pressed to a thin line, eyes blazing, nostrils flaring, and fists clenched, Fern straightened and tried storming outside to deal with the witch himself.

All the anger drained away when Artemis screamed Raphael's name, and the magic vanished like it never existed. Almost as if the witch was either out of this realm, or dead. A feral roar ripped from his chest as he forgot all about his pain and exhaustion and almost flew down the stairs.

Chapter Four

"I'm starting to regret killing Lazarus." Looking out the window, Artemis clenched her fists.

The world outside looked like a monochrome painting, with everything outlined in shades of gray and black. The few patches still not affected by whatever attacked the realm, stood out stark against it, pulling her focus as if taunting her. She felt Raphael behind her before he wrapped his arms around her waist pulling her to his chest.

"You are worried, and I agree with you on that. But, don't ever regret killing the bastard. Whatever is going on, I'm sure Lazarus had something to do with it. He was insane."

Turning around, Artemis pressed her face to Raphael's neck soaking up his strength and love. She knew he was right, but the guilt still gnawed inside her. She should've kept the asshole alive long enough to find out about the hidden portal or realms that he mentioned before he died. Every night her dreams replayed the last moments of their fight. Not wanting to worry Raphael any more, she kept it

The First Secret

to herself. She hasn't even told Ivy or Iris. After today's events, she wondered if she'd been mistaken.

"Do you want to tell me what's bothering you?" Raphael kissed the top of her head before leaning his cheek on it. "And don't tell me it's Lazarus; that's just your way of distracting me."

"I don't need words to distract you. All I have to do is take my clothes off." Her lips curled into a smile on the skin of his neck. Groaning he tightened his hold on her.

"I really didn't need to hear that," Iris grumbled from the bed. "I'm still in need of therapy after your bonding."

"Iris!" Artemis pushed Raphael aside making him growl under his breath and rushed to her side. "You are awake. How do you feel?"

"I swear I'm not trying to be a cockblock." Iris looked over her friend's shoulder at Raphael. "It's traumatic hearing you guys. I think that's what made Claude snap that night." Artemis snickered and glanced over her shoulder at her mate.

Another growl made Iris jerk her head to her right in alarm. Her breath froze in her lungs when she found Fern's stoic face. His clothes looked like he'd been crawling through thorn bushes for days and her stomach clenched at the thought. His hair hung wild and matted around his shoulders, and his face appeared painted for camouflage with dirt and mud. Only his dark sapphire eyes glowed as he stared at her intently. Warmth spread through her body at seeing him alive and unharmed.

"You made it back," she said. He pressed his lips tighter, remaining silent. Realizing he wasn't going to talk to her, not that she could blame him, Iris turned to Artemis. "Are you okay? How about Ivy?"

"I'm good, and Ivy woke up a few hours after we

brought her in." Reaching towards Iris, Artemis touched her face gently with her fingertips. "It's you that had us all worried. It's been two days. You haven't responded to anything or anyone." Raphael cleared his throat, and Artemis tilted her head. "Well, that's not true. You kept shaking and thrashing in the bed, but as soon as Fern was close, you calmed down. I guess that means you responded to something."

Heat rose in Iris's cheeks, and she kept her focus firmly on Artemis not daring to glance at the Fae staring holes in the side of her face. First, she couldn't wake him up, then she almost got him killed, and now he couldn't even rest, change his clothes, or shower because he had to keep watch over her. Tears prickled because she'd failed him and the rest of the people she liked to call friends. She swallowed the lump in her throat and braved looking at Fern again.

"I'm so..." she croaked, then cleared her throat. "I'm sorry." And she let him see her misery at letting him down. Fern's eyes widened, and their glow dimmed a little as his lips parted.

"I'll find a healer to check on you, and we will come back later; I think you two need to talk." Lifting herself off the bed where she had perched, Artemis grabbed Raphael's hand and pulled him towards the door.

"I think we all need to know what's going on—" Artemis put her hand over his mouth, cutting him off.

"I'll take my clothes off," she told him, and he almost dragged her out of the room. Artemis laughed and winked at Iris before closing the door behind her.

"I'm sorry," Iris repeated and braced herself for whatever anger or insults he could rightly throw at her.

"You keep saying you are sorry, but not what you are sorry about, witch." Fern's musical voice made her shiver under the covers. She couldn't meet his gaze. It felt as if it glided over her skin every time he spoke, which to her disappointment, or relief, didn't happen often.

"For everything?" She laughed humorlessly looking away from him, so she didn't have to see the confirmation of her failure. "For almost getting you killed, most of all." Her words were barely above a whisper.

"You had nothing to do with that." Her head snapped up. He looked disappointed as if he expected more from her.

"But... Claude... he was after me..." she stammered but trailed off when Fern made a cutting motion with his hand.

"The bloodsucker is after power. It doesn't matter to Claude if it's you, me, or someone else. You shouldn't be sorry for that, human." The way he said human, as if it was an insult, made her shrink back into the pillow as if he had slapped her. Confused, and taken aback, she stared at him.

Fern moved from where he leaned on the bedpost. Iris found it hard to breathe as he gracefully paced next to her bed. There was stiffness in his movements that she didn't miss, and guilt pinged in her chest.

"Have you told them that you are not human?" He glanced at her but didn't stop pacing making Iris feel dizzy.

"What are you talking about?" Anger bubbled in her chest, and all the guilt, or whatever it was that made her act timid, evaporated. "Of course I'm human, you stupid elf. Just because I have magic doesn't make me something else. Or is it a hard pill to swallow to know humans are more than just cattle?" Her voice rose with each word, and she practically shouted at the end.

"Don't call me that! I'm not some fairytale creature, and you better remember that when you're trying to irritate me." He snarled at her, and excitement at her ability to piss off this powerful being rose.

"What should I call you then?" Lifting both eyebrows, she blinked innocently at him. "A fairy? You do look feminine."

"There is nothing feminine about me, witch!" His breath warmed her lips when he got in her face and snarled. "I'm a Fae, not some make believe character humans write pretty stories about."

His scent filled her lungs making butterflies wrack havoc in her stomach. Her breath quickened. Iris wasn't sure what possessed her, and if anyone asked, she'd blame it on insanity or the fight with the shadow. Before she could think it through, she lifted her head and pressed her lips to his.

They both froze as a static-like current passed between them, and a sharp pain pierced her side and hip. Fern groaned and devoured her mouth sinking his hands in her hair making her forget everything else. She clawed at his back and shoulders to get closer as he pressed her to the mattress with his body. Delirious with passion, Iris's world closed down to Fern's animalistic growling and groaning.

"I'm so happy you are awake!" Ivy's gleeful voice caused Fern to push himself off her as if burned. Iris closed her eyes wishing she could disappear.

Chapter Five

"Oh, I'm sorry." Ivy looked anything but sorry as she waltzed inside the room with a smile. "Did I interrupt something?" She looked innocently at Fern, but he had his back turned and stood rigid staring out the window.

"No." Iris kept her voice cold and detached, burying the hurt at his embarrassment for being caught kissing her. Well technically he hadn't kissed her, she'd kissed him, but it's not like he resisted or moved away, Iris thought glumly.

"I'm not sure I'm okay because I'm acting out of character. I'm glad you came in before I did something stupid that I'll regret for the rest of my life."

Even from the corner of her eye, Iris saw Fern become so still that she wasn't sure the Fae was even breathing. Ivy's flinch at her words confused her even more, but Iris couldn't stop herself from lashing out at him for making her want to die of embarrassment at his rejection.

"She is not human!" Fern turned around, face devoid of any indication that her words have struck a chord.

"Okay," Ivy dragged the word while crawling on top of

the bed and getting comfortable next to Iris's legs. "I'll bite. What is she?"

"What do you mean, what is she?" Glaring, Fern folded his arms. "Whatever she is, it's not human!"

"Says you!" Iris snapped, glaring at him, but he ignored her. Something swirled in her chest, pressure built. Concentrating, she breathed slowly, pushing the magic down.

"Do you feel that?" Fern pointed an accusing finger at her. "No human can do that!"

"I don't feel anything." Ivy wore a small confused frown as she glanced between them. "What are you feeling?"

"Her magic!" A sneer twisted his face, and Iris's heart sunk to her toes at his disgust "It thickens the air every time she feels strong emotions."

"Is that what you were testing when I walked in?" Ivy glared at him, and Iris felt like hugging the woman.

"I'm telling you it's her magic!" he snarled at Ivy. "It's twisting us all around her little finger, the entire realm. All of us are running around trying to protect her and make her feel safe. Even Artemis for fuck sake. Are you blind? This will be a bigger disaster then Lazarus. Mark my words!"

Iris's thumb moved, touching the tips of her fingers. She squeezed her hands into fists so tight her nails broke the skin on her palms. 'Could he be telling the truth?' There was not enough oxygen in the room as panic gripped her, and she gasped for air like a fish out of water. 'Oh my god, I'm making them all act crazy, and I'll get them all killed,' her mind screamed as her eyes lost focus and she felt like she was drowning.

Ivy jumped off the bed yelling at Fern for being an idiot. Iris wished she could see the look on his face and laugh. Dark spots crept into her vision, and she stopped fighting

The First Secret

whatever was trying to kill her. Just as the pain in her chest became unbearable, two warm hands grabbed her face and tilted her head up. A face pressed to her neck, and a rush of air filled her lungs. Her body bowed off the bed almost throwing whoever it was off her. She kept gulping air with her eyes squeezed shut. A groan ripped from her every time she fought to expand her lungs against what felt like a boulder on the center of her chest. Bit by bit, it eased, and she finally relaxed enough to be able to breathe.

Fern couldn't remember the last time he'd experienced fear like the moment Iris's face turned almost blue, and she gaped like a fish, unable to breathe. And he thought he'd been scared when he thought she'd died in the courtyard two days ago. How wrong he'd been. Not knowing what to do and ignoring the screams and insults Ivy aimed at him, he grabbed her face in both hands and buried his face in her neck. Her skin was clammy while the floral scent he associated faded rapidly. He hated feeling helpless, and the witch kept making him feel like that every time he was around her. She started gulping air, almost dislodging him, but he held her tighter. Pulling back, he looked at her wide green eyes searching for anything to tell him what ailed her.

"Can you breathe?" he heard himself say, but he felt numb all over. Iris nodded stiffly, still wide-eyed and terrified. He turned his fear into anger and lashed out at Ivy.

"What the fuck is wrong with her?"

"Why do you care?" glaring at him, Ivy yanked him away from Iris and took his place checking her pulse and body temperature with the back of her hand.

"What's wrong with her, Dreamweaver? I'm in no mood for your games and riddles," he snarled, clenching his fists at his sides, so he didn't push Ivy away.

"You had one thing right, I'll give you that." Moving the

hair stuck to Iris's face and tucking it behind her ear, Ivy didn't look at Fern. "She is not human."

Iris jerked as if she'd been electrocuted at the words, and Fern pushed Ivy out of the way to cradle her to his chest. She calmed immediately, but his exhaustion meant that he could barely hold her to him.

"She is from the ancient line. Do you know what that means?"

"Artemis called me a changeling." Iris murmured through numb lips. She knew something was wrong with her, but she didn't know what.

"Artemis thinks you are half Fae?" Fern looked down at her frowning. Iris just shrugged a shoulder, or she tried. It only made her wiggle in Fern's lap. He gave her a warning glare.

"Well, yes and no," Ivy spoke slowly. Fern and Iris looked at her in shock.

"You mean you know what I am, and you didn't think it important to tell me?"

"Ivy now is the time to speak simply and clearly. No more half-truths." Fern made sure she saw he was tired of her bullshit.

"The ancient lines are more than just Fae." With a tired sigh, Ivy dropped into a chair next to the bed. "The Fae came from the ancient lines, just like humans, and every other species in all realms. The humans had it almost right when they called them gods." She looked solemn.

"What are you saying, Ivy?" Iris's heart stuttered. "My parents were human."

"Not really." Pressing her lips in a thin line Ivy looked at Iris with something resembling pity. "Where are your parents now?"

"They died when I was young…" her voice trailed off

when she realized she didn't have any distinct recollections f her parents. Just some vague memories that slipped through her fingers like water every time she tried to remember. "I've never seen my real parents, have I?" She looked at Ivy, and the other woman nodded slowly. Fern tightened his arms around her. She felt disconnected, as if watching herself from outside her body.

"They gave you a memory, just enough to keep you from searching." Standing up, Ivy took one of Iris's hands in both of hers. "They had to do it to keep you safe. Your kind were all hunted down and killed centuries ago. I can't believe you are in front of me. I thought all of you were gone until I found you in your dream. I did my best to protect you and keep your power bound, so you didn't attract attention. But eventually, you became stronger than me. That's when I made sure you met Artemis. It was the only way to keep you safe until you came here."

"And you used me to get what you wanted." Fern glared.

"So, what am I?" Holding her breath, Iris looked at Ivy.

"Your kind are known as the children of the Abyss, one of the creators, who give and take life. I'm not sure there is a word specific for what you are, as a name, or a title. The closest is the human word, god."

Iris stared at Ivy for long moments before a snort escaped her. She slapped a hand over her mouth to stop herself, but it was useless. Another snort followed, and a moment later she burst out laughing shaking Fern and the bed in the process. Tears streamed down her face from laughter, and her stomach ached. Fern and Ivy looked at each other confused at her reaction, but Iris couldn't stop laughing.

Chapter Six

"Has she been like this the whole time since you told her?" Artemis's brow pinched with worry as she spoke to Ivy. The other woman sat there staring at Iris while wringing her hands in her lap. She just nodded.

"A god!" Shaking her head, Iris kept giggling and bursting out into belly laughs as she'd been doing for the last couple of hours.

Fearing that the witch had finally lost her mind, Ivy had run to Artemis and Raphael while Fern stayed with Iris. She hoped that Iris would calm down soon so they could prepare. The way things were, Ivy wasn't sure if Iris was in any condition to leave the room, let alone go on a search for something that could be an object, a person, or a made-up tale.

"You should've waited for us if you were going to drop a bomb like that." Raphael frowned at Ivy.

"We don't have time to wait. Why aren't any of you listening is beyond me." Throwing up both hands, Ivy

The First Secret

retreated to the opposite side of the room pulling on her hair in frustration.

"You guys are nuts." Iris turned towards them, and they all stopped moving or talking. "Me," she pointed a finger at her chest, "a god!" She giggled again before taking a deep breath and wiping away the tears running down her cheeks.

"Are you calm now, so we can talk?" Artemis asked taking a half step towards her. Fern stood by Iris like some guardian ready to fight anyone who got near while she tried to deal with whatever was happening to her.

"Listen to me!" All humor gone, Iris begged Artemis to see reason. "Most days I can't tell the difference between my right and left shoes. I wear dresses because I'm worried that if I try something else, I'd end up in mismatched clothing and look like a lunatic. On my best days, I can barely control my magic, and everyone stays away from me because they think I'm either weird or scary." She looked at each of them in turn. "Even Danny, the girl who works for me, keeps her distance. And you're telling me I'm a direct bloodline from gods? You do realize how crazy that sounds, right?" Looking hopefully at Artemis, Iris nodded as if encouraging the other woman to agree. "Right?"

"Iris, how have your relationships been throughout your life?" Ivy's gentle question made Iris frown.

"What's that got to do with anything?"

"Humor me." Waving her hand in encouragement, Ivy looked at her expectantly.

"Umm..." Clearing her throat, Iris sensed Fern's focus on her. If she were lucky the ground would open and swallow her, so she didn't have to answer. It didn't happen, so she cleared her throat again before focusing on Ivy and pretending they were alone. "Never good. The few ones I tried to have anyway."

"Why?"

"I don't know. Because I'm attracted to assholes? Who knows." Unable to sit still Iris started pacing. "It's always nice at the beginning. Maybe, too nice. After a month or so they become clingy, insecure, and try to lock me in a cage of their needs and expectations. I found it suffocating and stressful, so I stopped even trying after a couple of times dealing with the same thing."

"And friends?" Ivy kept going.

"Why is this important, Ivy?" Artemis said as Ivy continued pacing.

"I've never had friends. Whenever I tried to be friends with someone, they always needed something from me to have that friendship. Either helping them with something, or to get closer to someone else, and I had to make it happen. Or they were bored at the time…who knows." Agitated, she cocked her hip placing her hand on it. "Not that I give a damn. I like my solitude, thank you very much."

"You have friends," Artemis spoke up, and grabbing Iris's arm, she pulled her into a hug. It took a second for Iris to return it.. Artemis was not a touchy-feely person.

"Yes, witch! You have friends, even when some of them don't know how to show it." Raphael smiled sheepishly at her, and warmth spread in Iris's chest.

"Aww, you guys! It's my winning personality, I just know it!" Iris deadpanned. They all chuckled, and the awkward emotional moment relaxed.

"I wouldn't go that far, human." Fern nudged her with his shoulder and Iris tried not to show how much it affected her.

"Of course, you wouldn't, elf." She stuck her tongue at him. Everyone laughed, but Fern zeroed in on her mouth, and when his gaze locked again on hers the undeniable hunger there made her shift uncomfortably.

"All that happened because of who you are." Ivy killed the little joy that had crawled back inside Iris. She just couldn't leave the talk alone. "Humans act possessively because your magic makes them feel good." Iris frowned, and Ivy continued her explanation. "Subconsciously, your magic, who you are, made them feel good, happy. When you give your full attention to someone, if you are in a good mood, it feeds them happiness and life. Humans become addicted to it, so they crave it and become obsessed if they don't have a constant supply. They turn possessive and controlling. That only makes you unhappy and feeds their misery. It's a double-edged sword, but you are a creator after all."

Iris thought about the couple of men she'd dated and the changes in their behavior. Ivy's words were the closest thing to an explanation she had ever heard. Could it be that it wasn't her pushing people away or her being hard to be with? Could the answer to her misery be in her genetics?

"You guys are not acting like that." Iris gave last-ditch effort to argue the point. "Fern even hates my guts. My magic disgusts him."

"What?" Fern pulled back like she had punched him and looked at her incredulously. "I don't hate you!"

"Mhm, could've fooled me, elf." It was apparent by the look on her face she didn't believe him, and his heart sank.

"Come," Ivy grabbed Iris's hand and dragged her out of the room. "Let me show you something." Artemis and Raphael followed, but Fern couldn't move from the spot.

"Artemis," he called, and both her and Raphael looked back at him. "Can I have a word... please." Her eyebrows hit her hairline and he grimaced. "I've said please before."

"What's wrong?" After pushing Raphael out of the room, she returned to Fern.

"I think I fucked up."

"What's new?" she crossed her arms looking down her nose. He ground his teeth.

"I fucked up with the witch. There is just something about her that makes me irrational. It makes me… I don't know what it makes me. Help me fix it? You can gloat later."

"I never thought I'll see the day." A wicked smile bloomed on her face, and he groaned. "You will owe me big time for this!"

Chapter Seven

"Why are we here?" Looking around anxiously, Iris tried not to show how freaked out she was at being in the same spot where the shadow attacked them.

"Breathe, witch. I won't let anything happen to you. Artemis will be very upset if you get hurt on my watch." Raphael patted her shoulder awkwardly.

"Thanks, boss man." She gave him a tight smile acknowledging his effort even though he was weird around people. He beamed at her proudly, and she couldn't help but chuckle.

"Look!" Ivy almost vibrated in excitement, pointing at the lawn.

"I see nothing." Iris looked at Raphael for help, but the vampire looked just as confused. It was still strange to see him standing outside in daylight, but in this realm, it didn't seem to bother him.

"Look down, Iris. Look at the grass." Ivy pointed, bouncing on her toes like a child.

Following Ivy's finger, a frown formed on Iris's face

before her stomach dropped. A small circle of blackened earth stood out in the middle of the lush green grass like a sore thumb.

"Is that..." Iris felt faint. "Did I do that?"

"Yes!" Ivy's smile was so big Iris couldn't help staring at her openmouthed. "When you were scared you took life!"

"I'm not much of a people person, but even I know that's not how you go about it," Raphael muttered under his breath rubbing his hands over his face.

"This is proof!" Ivy glared at him. "She is a creator. If she can take life from this realm, she can also give it!"

"Hold on just a minute!" Iris took a few steps away from Ivy. "You want me to give life to what exactly?"

"To the realm, of course." Ivy looked at her as if she was stupid for not getting it straight away.

"The entire realm?" The Fae were all crazy. "How exactly do you expect me to do that? Should I walk around pointing at things telling them to live?"

"There is no reason to be a smartass," Ivy told her primly. Raphael snorted covering it with a cough. Iris glared at him. Flicking her fingers, she zapped him with a current of electricity making him bare his fangs at her.

"See, it comes so naturally for you to manipulate the energy around you. You just need to find the first secret, and you'll know how to help us."

"Where do I find it? Is it written somewhere? Do I need to do research in the library? Because I'm totally up for that." Iris perked up at the idea of hiding behind books from everyone, especially Fern.

"No." her heart sank at Ivy's words. "From what I've glimpsed and what Lazarus told Artemis before he died, you need to go to the caves. That's where you'll find it."

"What caves? And your face when you mention them is

not giving me the warm fuzzies to go there, just so you know."

"I don't think Artemis will be happy with this information." Raphael pointed out, folding his arms, and Iris wanted to hug him for it. She did not want to go to any caves.

"It's a good thing it's not up to her now is it?" Placing both hands on her hips, Ivy glowed brighter.

Iris's head ached from all the crazy going on around her non-stop. Her temples throbbed, and it felt like someone was sticking icepicks at the back of her eyeballs. Taking a deep breath, she held it in as long as she could before releasing it slowly in hopes of not emptying her stomach where she stood. She felt his presence before she heard his footsteps. It was almost as if they were connected by some unseen cord.

"Are you okay?" Fern's voice washed over her. His warm palm wrapped around her arm and the headache disappeared like it had never existed. Alarms flared up inside Iris.

"Peachy." Pulling her arm from him, she stepped away making him frown. "I need to go to some caves then give life to an entire realm. A walk in the park, right?" She smiled tightly giving him a thumbs up.

"What did you do to her?" Fern whirled on Ivy and Raphael. "She seemed better, now you've broken her again. She doesn't make sense."

"Whoa, there buddy! I'm standing right here so don't talk about me like I'm some kind of an idiot." Glaring, Iris pointed a finger in his face. "And I have no obligation to make sense to you! So, mind your own business. Go play with the other elves or something."

"Damn, you even make me look good when you open your mouth." Raphael laughed at Fern's confused face.

"They say I'm bullheaded and not very observant, but you, my friend, take the gold on that one."

"What did I miss?" Artemis walked over, and Raphael pulled her to his side, wrapping his arms around her.

"What do you call it?" He tilted his head left and right as if thinking. "Aha! Yes! You missed Fern putting his foot in his mouth." Even Iris and Ivy chuckled at Raphael's excitement.

"According to Ivy, I need to go to some caves and find the first secret." Iris repeated everything that Ivy had said. Artemis listened intently, unblinkingly, making Iris feel better about the whole thing. At least one of them didn't think she was weird or crazy. "So, I guess that's the only way to help your realm, and I think I owe you that much for keeping me here away from Claude. I have no other choice but to go. I'm just not sure everything Ivy is hoping is true, will be the actual truth. I don't want to disappoint anyone."

"Iris." Pulling herself away from her mate, Artemis placed both hands on Iris's shoulders. "You have been through so much ever since Raphael found you, even before that with Ivy visiting your dreams. I've never had a high opinion of humans, but you changed that. If anyone can do this, there is no doubt in my mind that it will be you. You are a loyal friend and a strong woman. I don't have to think twice about placing the fate of my realm and my people in your hands because you have proven yourself worthy of that trust. There is nothing you can't do if you set your mind to it and you will never, ever disappoint me unless you give up on yourself and who you are."

"Thank you!" Iris choked the words out and wrapped her arms around Artemis. She couldn't stop the tears that trickled down her cheeks, and she didn't want to.

The First Secret

"She can't go by herself," Ivy started, but Fern was already speaking over her.

"I'm going with her." Crossing his arms over his chest, he glared at all of them as if daring them to try and stop him.

"You are going regardless." Ivy dismissed him, but Iris jerked her head away from Artemis's shoulder to glare at the Dreamweaver.

"What do you mean, he is going? No, he is not!"

"After you passed out from holding the shield against the shadow the only thing making you calm down and get better is his presence. He is going." Ivy's voice allowed no argument.

Iris thought back from the time she woke up until just now when she had the headache standing in the grass. A sinking feeling told her Ivy was right because every time she experienced pain or panic, only Fern calmed her down and stopped the pain.

"Maybe it's because I kept him alive in my realm. My magic could've connected with him somehow." She searched Ivy's face for anything to deny her words but found nothing.

"Whatever it is, I'm sure we can fix it after you come back. I'll do everything I can to help." Artemis told her, and Iris felt better instantly. She would find a way not to depend on the Fae, especially since he couldn't stand her.

"Okay, let's get ready and go." Iris started walking towards the palace not waiting on anyone.

"Now?" Fern was right on her heels as if she'd escape if he couldn't see her.

"The sooner I go, the sooner this crap fest will be over. No time like the present," Iris told him over her shoulder, and they both disappeared through the double doors.

"That was very nice of you to tell her that. She needed to hear it." Ivy walked up and stood next to Artemis. "I thought she'd refuse to even try."

"If anything happens to her in those caves, or she doesn't come back," Artemis locked her violet glowing eyes on Ivy's, and Ivy shivered at the promise she saw there. "I will kill you."

With those words, Artemis grabbed Raphael's hand, and they strode towards the palace, leaving Ivy watching their retreating backs. She prayed with all that she had that she hadn't made a mistake by sending Iris to the caves so soon. Maybe she should've waited until later, but too late for second guessing now. As things were, they'll either all be saved, or Ivy's days were numbered. There was no doubt in her mind that Artemis would keep her promise.

Chapter Eight

The knock on the door pulled Iris from the internal panic that she was fighting. Sitting on the edge of the large bed with her face in her hands, she was trying her best to get in a positive mindset about this whole cave business. She hated closed spaces. Even more, she hated dark closed areas, especially caves. They made her feel like she was buried alive and she was willing to do anything not to put herself in that kind of situation. Well, almost anything. Letting down people who counted on her was not one of them.

The knock came again. Groaning, she lifted her head and pushed herself off the bed. With cold, sweaty hands she reached for the door knowing it was probably Fern asking her if she was ready. She was so not ready, but she'd never tell anyone that.

Yanking the door open, all she could do was blink slowly. Twice. At first glance, she thought Fern stood at her door. The angular face with a straight nose and full lips that a woman could die for along with the same shiny long black hair. The tips of the pointy ears sticking up through the silky strands were the same, too. Her gaze traveled from black leather boots, up the muscular thighs wrapped in black fabric, to a trim waist and chiseled bare torso that looked like it was painted from a woman's wild wet dreams. Then her gaze locked on citrine eyes that looked at her with curiosity and amusement.

She snapped her out of her stupefied state. Her hip and the side of her waist jabbed with burning pain. She hissed and took a step back from the Fae standing at her door.

"Are you okay, human?" the Fae spoke in that musical quality voice they all possessed and reached a hand to catch her if she stumbled. Iris took another step back.

"Who are you?" Suspicion gnawed at her, and she shook her hands preparing to blast him to kingdom come if he tried anything. "And what do you want?" She couldn't explain her unease. She wanted nothing else but for him to go away.

"Oh." Chuckling and shifting uncomfortably he looked at her through thick lashes as if embarrassed. It confused the hell out of her, especially after his reaction when she saw him at her door. "My name is Darion. Artemis sent me to give you this." Thrusting his hands towards her and making her flinch, which she hated, made her realize he was holding a bundle of clothing. he was offering her like some holy sacrifice. Iris had no idea how she missed it.

"Umm…" Shaking her head, feeling confused at her reaction, she snatched the clothing from his hands as if he might bite her. "Thanks." Giving him a tight, uncomfortable smile, which probably looked more like a grimace, she hugged the clothing to her chest like a shield.

"We'll be leaving in few blinks, so I'll leave and wait in the courtyard. Meet us there when you're ready."

The First Secret

"Ah, I'm sorry, we?" Darion was turning to leave, but her words stopped him midturn.

"Yes! I'm coming with you to the caves." He gave her a bright, excited smile that would've made another woman swoon, but Iris felt like she was going to faint. "Don't worry, I'm an excellent guide and tracker. I'll get us all there in no time." Darion gave her a reassuring smile leaving her to stare at the muscles on his back bunching and twitching with his movements as he walked away.

"What the hell was that?" Groaning, Iris buried her face in the bundle of clothing. "Well, at least I won't be alone with Fern, so there is that," she murmured before closing the door so she could get ready.

Standing in the hallway not far from the room, Fern seethed with his fist clenched at his sides. He'd gotten ready as fast as he could, dressing in a hurry, yanking strands off his hair trying to brush it quickly so he could return to Iris to make sure she was okay. When he saw Darion knocking on her door, like a coward, he slipped behind one of the statues Lazarus had left all over the place before he died.

He and Darion had been friends since they were younglings and he considered him a brother. Neither had families and they were raised for the hunt. Never in his long life did Fern think that he would hate the other male, but at the moment he wanted nothing more than to wring his neck. His heart beat faster at Iris's reaction until Darion said that he would be going with them. He had seen his friend around women, and they were never able to resist him for long. Darion was easy going and funny, everything Fern was not. And now he would be close to Iris for the fates knew how long. Still fighting his feelings, Fern convinced himself that he only cared that the witch lived and was safe because she might be able to heal his realm and help his people. He had no other reason to care about her at all. She was an abomination that shouldn't even exist. Still, unable to help himself, he rushed after Darion.

"Darion, hey!" Jogging up behind his friend he slapped him on the back. "Where are you going?"

"Didn't Artemis tell you?" Darion gave him a huge smile not slowing his stride. "I'm going with you! And the human." He wiggled his eyebrows, excitement evident on his face.

"No, she didn't." Fern couldn't keep the bitterness from his voice. "I didn't think we needed help; I'm enough protection for a human."

"No offense meant, my friend. I think she was worried because of everything you've been through lately. There is no harm in having someone watch your back." Darion looked so earnest and apologetic that guilt stabbed Fern's gut. "Besides, no one's been in those caves in centuries, as far as I know. Who knows what we'll find there?"

"That's a good point." Slapping Darion on the back one more time and giving him a strained smile, Fern changed direction calling over his shoulder. "I'll meet you in the courtyard, I forgot something."

Nodding, Darion continued down the broad stairway while Fern, in his anger, almost sprinted to Raphael's and Artemis's room. Without knocking, feeling like a man possessed, he barged in making the heavy door bang off the wall and almost hit his shoulder on the way back. His arm shot out, and his palm slapped hard stopping the large piece of wood from knocking him off his feet. Raphael was leaning his back on the large window with his arms crossed over his chest. Artemis stood, proud and regal in the middle of the room, violet eyes glowing, with her purple hair falling

The First Secret

like a curtain down her back with her hands on her hips as if waiting for him. They stared at each other for few moments until she lifted one of her eyebrows daring him to speak.

"He is not going!" Fern flinched internally at the way he snapped at her, but he was beyond reason or logic when it came to Iris.

"Who is not going?" It sounded like Artemis was suppressing laughter and it pissed him off even more. Raphael sounded like he was choking then he placed his fist over his mouth and coughed. Fern couldn't care less at this point.

"Darion!" Swinging his hand in a cutting motion, he puffed up his chest. "He is not going. I don't need him."

"It's a good thing that it's not up to you then, is it?" Glaring, Artemis kept her intimidating gaze on him. "You might not need him, but Iris does if she is to be safe. He is going."

"Fine, find someone else then. Not Darion."

"He is the best tracker, Fern." She tried to reason with him, but he was a long way from listening.

"I am the best tracker after you!"

"And you are going, aren't you?"

"I thought I asked you to help." Fern snarled. She smiled and his gut twisted. She enjoyed seeing him like this. Still, he couldn't control his anger.

"I am helping you. You're just too ignorant and stubborn to see it."

"You don't understand!" he tried pleading. "I can't look after them both. If Darion goes, and it's not just me, the human will die."

Shaking her head like he disappointed her, Artemis

closed her eyes with a sigh. Fern opened his mouth to keep talking, but a loud gasp behind him made all the blood drain from his face. Raphael groaned as if in pain and tapped the back of his head on the window.

Chapter Nine

Iris wiped her hands on her thighs as she stared in the mirror. It was almost like she'd forgotten how she looked when wearing anything but a dress.

The flat knee-high leather boots felt as comfortable as being barefoot and the soft fabric of her pants was unlike anything she had seen or touched before. It had an almost silky feel, but it looked like cotton. Whatever it was, it was so comfortable that, she was sure that she'd never want to take the pants off. At first, Iris wasn't so sure about the corset that Artemis sent her, but after thinking about it, she decided that her friend knew best. The weather remained hot and walking for an extended period will make it feel even warmer.

She needed to talk to Artemis before they left. Dark hair floated around her pale face, and her green eyes stared back at her wide and worried. Iris looked at the low waist of her pants and the golden glowing symbols that had appeared on her skin. She wracked her brain for when it could've happened, but apart from that burning sensation when

Darion had appeared at her door, Iris couldn't recall another instance. That's not to say it couldn't have happened sooner. She'd had one shock after another ever since Raphael waltzed into her store and considered herself lucky for remembering her own name at the moment.

Grabbing the cloak hanging on the side of the tall mirror, she headed to see Artemis. If anyone would know what these symbols meant, and why they had mysteriously appeared on her body, it'll be either Artemis or Ivy. Iris felt more in the mood to see her friend than Ivy, so she hurried towards her friend's rooms. When she neared the room, a male voice she would recognize anywhere floated through the open doors.

"...the human will die!" Fern snarled. Iris couldn't hide the gasp that echoed in the empty hallway.

Not wanting to be seen, or see the jerk elf, and forgetting everything about glowing symbols, Iris ran towards the courtyard. The asshole didn't think she could keep herself alive, let alone help his realm. It was like a slap in the face, and everything blurred from the unshed tears. Fae stopped in their tracks to watch her almost fly by them in her rush to get out of the palace. Her hair trailed behind her like a dark flag, the cloak catching on a statue made her stumble, but she didn't stop until she burst through the front doors and plowed straight into Darion almost causing them both topple to the ground.

"Whoa there human." Wrapping his arms around her, Darion stumbled but somehow managed to hold them both up. "What's the hurry? I wasn't going to leave without you." Giving her a charming smile, he kept his arms around her.

Iris couldn't answer, pull away, or even straighten up as pain lanced her hip. She kept her lips pressed firmly because if she dared to move, she knew that she'd empty her stomach all over Darion. Nostrils flaring, she did her best to push down the bile rising in her throat, squeezing her eyes shut while tears streamed down her face.

"What's wrong?" Darion changed from a charming guy into a warrior who would've made her shiver in fear if she'd been able to do anything else but breathe through her nose.

Squaring his shoulders, and pulling out wicked looking short swords, he pushed her behind him bending his knees as if bracing for an attack.

Iris wanted to tell him that nothing was wrong, but she could only whimper and wrap her arms around her middle bending down from the burning pain. Even though her whole body felt stiff as a rock and her arms were tightly wrapped around her, her thumb moved to touch the tips of her fingers. The heat of magic started building at the center of her chest, and Iris couldn't even warn Darion to run away. 'Please, no, no, noooo' she screamed in her head 'I don't want to hurt him,' but it was too late. A blast erupted from her. Slamming into Darion's back, it sent him flying away until he skidded to a stop couple of yards away.

The burning on her hip lessened, then slowly faded into nothing, leaving her nerves frayed and mind confused. Why was this happening to her? Finally able to straighten up, Iris took a much-needed deep breath and turned to see if the poor Fae was okay. A sound between a growl and a groan coming from the palace doors stopped her in her tracks. First, she squinted, then shock hit her as Fern lifted himself off the ground where he was apparently sprawled, and his glowing sapphire eyes locked on hers. His long black hair was mused and looked wild, making him more breathtaking than he had any right to be. Iris opened her mouth to ask him if he was okay or apologize, she wasn't sure which, but then remembered why she'd run outside. Giving him a glare that made him look at her startled, she turned her back on him and stomped towards Darion.

"Serves you right, jerk," she muttered under her breath.

Walking as close as she dared to Darion, Iris's concern rose. He lay face down in the dirt his arms and legs flung around him, unmoving. The last thing she needed was to kill one of the Fae, while they were keeping her safe here from Claude. Although If she'd killed Darion, the crazy vampire king would be the least of her worries. Her heart beat again as Darion groaned and flipped on his back peering up at her through thick lashes.

"Oh, good! You're fine!" Sounding a little too chirpy to her own ears and clapping her hands like some kindergarten teacher, she straightened up and looked around. "Let's go then!" not wanting him to see how freaked out she was, Iris started walking in a random direction.

"The human is strange," Darion groaned, but she kept walking.

"Yeah, she is something," Fern replied, much closer than she expected him to be. "You are going in the wrong direction," he called out to her.

Not missing a beat, she flipped around and ignoring them both started walking back towards them. As she neared to where they were standing and watching her, she lifted her chin stubbornly and tried to walk by them, but Fern grabbed hold of her cloak and steered her in the direction they needed to go. She hadn't been headed that way the second time either, but she'd be damned if she told him that.

"I knew that!" Iris sniffed and stomped towards the gray horizon stretching in front of her. She heard the two men chuckle behind her, but she did her best to ignore them. Well, until they spoke.

"Who angered the human?" Darion asked.

"Who angered the human?" Iris mimicked, mocking Darion's voice. "The human has a name. It's Iris." Glaring over her shoulder at him, she lifted her chin. "You better start using it, or I'll send your ass flying again. See how you like that!"

Fern's laugh boomed and echoed behind her, and no matter how hurt or upset she was with him, Iris couldn't stop her lips twitching before they lifted at the corners in a smile. She was just happy the jerk elf didn't see it. Calling him elf even in her own head when she knew how much he hated it made her snicker.

"I have a feeling that sound she made is not a good thing," Darion observed, and this time she couldn't help but laugh.

Chapter Ten

Fern kept his focus centered on Iris as she walked a few paces in front of him and Darion. After whatever had made her magic flare up in front of the palace, she ignored them both completely. He wasn't sure what she'd heard, and his gut twisted to think that she now thought he was just like those controlling and possessive humans her and Ivy spoke about. No, Fern decided, he wasn't like them at all. He only wanted the witch to stay safe and alive to save his realm. Keeping Darion away from her was part of that too and not because he cared if she fell for his friend's charms.

The longer they walked through the barren grayness, the more his heart hurt for all the perished beauty and nature. Amongst all the dead gray land, Iris stood out like an oasis in a desert. Like something you should worship. He clenched his fists and changed his line of thinking. To this day, Fern didn't know how none of them had noticed their realm declining. Had Lazarus placed some sort of illusion to blind them to the damage and destruction he brought, or were his kind really as arrogant and full of themselves as

The First Secret

Raphael and Iris had pointed out more than once? So lost in his own thoughts and drowning in guilt for letting Lazarus guide him around like a fool, Fern didn't notice that Darion had jogged the few paces to catch up with Iris until he heard him talk.

"You're feeling better now, Iris?" Darion gave her a disarming smile. She turned to look at him when he said her name for the first time, and he shrugged, looking apologetic. "Thank you for telling me your name."

Iris searched his face for some sign of him trying to be a smartass but found his expression open, friendly, and pleading for forgiveness. Keeping her distance in case the pain from her hip hit again, she glanced over her shoulder at Fern. She wondered what game he was playing by sending Darion to talk to her, but one look at him told her he wasn't happy about it either. Jaw clenched, he looked ready to rip a stone apart with his bare hands. Darion cleared his throat, and Iris looked away from Fern.

"You're welcome, and yes, I do feel better. I have no idea what happened back there." Looking in front of her, so he doesn't see her confusion at Fern's reaction, Iris exhaled a deep sigh. "You know, when any of you call me human, you make the word sound like something bad, or useless." Glancing at Darion from the corner of her eye she saw his lips part in shock. "I'm not saying you mean it that way. Well…" she tilted her head left and right as if debating. "… not all of you, let's say. Anyway, it makes me feel like you see me lower than the dirt on your boot. It's not a nice feeling, I can tell you that much."

"I'm sorry." Sincerity shone in Darion's voice. "I never meant it like that. To us, to me, saying human is like when a youngling has a new toy." When Iris looked at him sharply, he backpaddled. "the word I mean. Using it. It's new, and I have never seen one...a human. It never occurred to me that it might sound insulting to you. For my part in making you feel like that, I'm truly sorry."

Fern snorted behind them, and Iris turned to glare at him over her shoulder. She couldn't help wondering why he had to be such a jerk all the time. Iris hasn't done anything to him personally. Okay, she'd almost got him killed, but that was beside the point. It's not like she wanted Claude to kill them both. So, why the hell did he hate her so much? And what's worse, why did she feel this pull that made her melt every time she looked at him? It was obvious that she'd told Ivy the truth. She really was only attracted to assholes.

Iris realized that she hadn't replied to Darion in longer than was polite, so she turned and gave him a rare, genuine smile.

"Thank you, Darion." His smile slipped, and his lips parted as if seeing her for the first time. A frown pulled her eyebrows together, and she lost her smile. "You are forgiven," she told him awkwardly and speed up to put as much distance as she could between them.

Fern believed that finally, his heart was as numb as his fingers were from clenching them tightly. The smile that lit up Iris's face felt like the sun had turned all its attention to whoever received it. He saw the change in Darion as well when his friend gaped at her, stupefied. Fern itched to punch him in the face. The witch would be the death of him. Her hair bounced around her shoulders in sync with her pert little ass when she walked faster, putting distance between her and Darion. The red haze he was in subsided.

"I would help you close your mouth, but I don't know who will close mine," Darion spoke from next to him. Fern hadn't even noticed his friend. The witch would definitely be the death of him if he didn't start paying attention.

The First Secret

"You should keep your distance," Fern told him curtly. Darion's eyebrows hit his hairline.

"Is that how things are?" He looked more closely at Fern and couldn't believe he hadn't noticed his stiff posture until now.

"There are no things. Don't be stupid, Darion." Fern turned his sapphire eyes towards him. "We know nothing about her, or what she really is. Keeping our distance is the smart thing to do, or we might end up with another Lazarus on our hands."

"Dear fates you have lost your mind." Darion looked at him incredulously. "You actually believe the bullshit coming out of your mouth right now." Throwing his head back, Darion stopped in his tracks and roared in laughter. He even slapped his thigh few times and tears glistened on his lashes before sliding down his cheeks.

"It looks to me like I'm the only one who hasn't lost their mind. All of you, even Ivy and Artemis, run around like pups to her every whim." Snarling, Fern sped up. Darion laughed louder.

"It looks to me that you like the hu…Iris." Jogging up to Fern, Darion corrected himself before using the word that made Iris uncomfortable. "Maybe more than like, huh, old friend?"

"You don't know what you're talking about." Not slowing down Fern kept walking.

"Oh, I know what I'm talking about, I assure you. I just didn't think I'd see the day." Chuckling, Darion kept pace with him.

"You sound like Artemis."

"And she is a brilliant woman if she saw through your bullshit sooner than the rest of us." Those words earned

Darion a glare promising pain, but he smiled even brighter at Fern.

"Let's catch her before the witch gets herself killed."

With a clenched jaw, Fern broke into a jog after Iris, and her head turned to look back over her shoulder as if she could sense him moving closer.

'What an interesting reaction' Darion thought to himself, and keeping his smile, he followed Fern.

"This is going to be an exciting adventure." He chuckled under his breath.

Chapter Eleven

The heat was getting unbearable as the three of them continued walking with no end in sight. The scenery blurred, and Iris rubbed at her eyes in hopes of relieving the dryness that made them itchy. A movement to her right got her attention, but she had to blink a few times to realize that Darion proffered a flask of water. She hadn't drunk anything since before they left the palace. With a grateful smile, she took it and sipped slowly. The cold water felt heavenly as it cooled her parched throat.

"I know it seems like there is no end to the walking, but we should be able to see the hills soon," Fern spoke from her other side making her glance at him.

He'd been quiet ever since Darion laughed at whatever he'd said. Was it an hour ago? A few hours ago? Iris had no idea how long they've been walking. The only thing she knew was that her legs were about to give out on her. The way her hair stuck to her face annoyed her, and she flapped the cloak to get some sort of a breeze on her skin.

"Do you want to stop and rest?" Darion offered, but she shook her head and kept walking.

"I will not be the weakest link," she told him, her voice raspy from being quiet for so long.

"A what?" Fern turned towards her, but Iris stared straight just so she didn't have to look at him.

She felt his nearness way too keenly for her liking, almost as if her body was aware of his location at all times. It wreaked havoc on her hormones and her mind. If she looked at his face, she was worried she might start drooling like some idiot, so to be safe she didn't even glance.

"The weakest link, you know?" Waving her hand, she concentrated on putting one foot in front of the other. "They ask questions, and you try to answer them the best you can. If you get it right, you help your team. If you keep getting things wrong, you are the weakest link. Sometimes they even flush them down a tube." She snickered remembering watching that show.

"Maybe we should stop," Darion spoke to Fern over her head. "I think she is hallucinating and talking nonsense."

"She is talking about some human things." After watching her for long moments, Fern added, "It is not a bad thing to stop, Iris. We all need to rest for a blink."

She shivered when Fern said her name. It sounded exotic and beautiful when spoken in his deep musical voice, and she looked at him. His sapphire gaze traced her face as if he expected her to pass out at any moment. He wasn't far from the truth, but somewhere along the way, Iris had convinced herself that she must not show weakness. They expected her to save an entire realm after all. She would get to those damn caves even if she had to claw her way there.

"It doesn't look like the two of you need rest." She stumbled almost tripping over her own feet. Fern grabbed her arm to steady her. "I'm fine." Jerking her arm away, she continued walking. "I can walk."

"Iris, stop!" Grabbing her arm again, Fern yanked her to his chest. "It's not a weakness to stop for a blink." Looking up at him, her heart leaped in her throat. "I swear it." All Iris could do was blink. "And I will not flush you down a tube. You have my word." His lips twitched before he smiled tentatively.

"Darion?"

Fern frowned and dropped his smile when she called to the other Fae. Darion popped his head into her line of sight. "I think you were right. I'm hallucinating." Iris kept staring at Fern and at her words his lips curved into a beautiful smile.

"Or maybe the heat got to Fern's head, and he is delirious." Darion chuckled and scanned the area for a place to rest.

The dead, leafless trees were sparse, but there was some close by that they could use for shade. Indicating one with a broader trunk then the rest, Darion headed towards it. Iris tried to turn and follow, but before she even pushed herself away from Fern, he scooped her up in his arms. Not giving her time to argue or wiggle out of his hold, he followed Darion with determined steps.

Iris couldn't work him out. One moment, Fern acted as if he couldn't help himself and all he wanted to do was touch her, the next he was a jerk who appeared to hate her more than anything in the world. She stared at his profile as he walked them over to the tree. The thick lashes mesmerized her with each slow blink he took. Or maybe she really was delirious, because she felt drunk. Fern passed Darion, using longer strides and Iris looked over his shoulder. Darion slowed his steps and winked at her with a big smile on his face.

"He is bipolar," Iris blurted out. The connection from her mouth to her brain seemed to have been cut.

"He is what?" Darion walked closer so he could look at her closely. He even squinted as if that will help him see better.

"One minute he smiles at me and carries me around like some Snow White crap. The next, he looks like he wants to be the one to end my life." Iris chuckled shaking her head, and Fern's steps faltered before he resumed walking. "Bipolar, I'm telling you."

"I do not want to end your life." Fern's low voice sobered her up. "I want you to live." Stopping at the tree, he held her in his arms longer than needed before kneeling down and placing her on the ground. "We will rest for a blink, then continue. It's not that far now, we're past the halfway point."

Dropping on the ground next to her, he stretched his long legs out, folded his arms behind his head and closed his eyes. He looked like a statue to Iris. Darion patrolled the area, so Iris found herself observing Fern without feeling awkward. It was just like when he'd been unconscious at the store. She almost reached out a finger to trace his jaw, but he opened one eye and peered at her.

"What do you think we will find at those caves?" Trying to hide her rising blush, she figured the caves were a safe subject. As if hearing her, even though he was far enough not to have done, Darion headed back.

"I don't know." Opening the other eye as well, Fern turned towards her. "No one but Lazarus was allowed inside. I tried once, but he had some protection placed around them. I couldn't break it."

"I've heard a few of the warriors mention that they tried as well on a dare." Dropping on the ground close to them, Darion joined the conversation. "None of them were able to enter."

"But now we can, right?" She looked from one frowning face to the other.

"All the other wards and protections that Lazarus set are broken now that he is dead." Fern looked at Darion for confirmation, and the other Fae nodded. "This shouldn't be any different."

"Well, that sounds promising." Rubbing her calves, Iris couldn't help worrying. "If not, we will have come all this way for nothing."

"If there is still anything around the caves, I'm sure your magic will break it." Fern sounded a hell of a lot more confident in her magic than her.

"You shouldn't worry about that now, Iris," Darion said. "We need to get there first. After that, we will deal with whatever we need to deal with."

"I'm not worried that much about getting in," she mumbled, and both men looked at her with a strange expression on their faces.

"What did you say?" Fern looked at her intently, and she squirmed.

"I said, I'm not worried that much about getting inside the cave." Taking a deep breath, she released it slowly. "I'm more worried about what we will find when we do get in."

Chapter Twelve

Knowing that they won't be staying long under the shade of the dead tree, Iris closed her eyes leaning against the thick trunk to avoid the Fae's intense stare more than anything else.

Even like this, she was very aware of Fern's nearness, like her body was connected to his in ways she couldn't explain. Iris had never felt anything like this before, and it made her jittery and anxious that she wasn't sure if she wanted to be closer to him or run away and hide until it went away. He clearly wanted nothing to do with her, and all the times he was nice or protective of her must be because he hoped that she might save his realm. Or maybe he had some misguided obligation because she helped him survive when he broke the oath to Lazarus that should've killed him.

Iris still didn't know how her magic had kept his heart beating, but she was grateful regardless. Fern might be a jerk elf, but it'll be a shame if that pretty face no longer graced the worlds with its presence. Opening one eye slightly, she cast a sideways glance at him.

Fern was trying his best to not grab Iris and drag her into his lap to just hold her for a second. The witch was stubborn as all hell, but no matter how hard she tried to act tough he could see the slight slope of her shoulders and the way her legs moved slower the longer they walked. At first, he thought Iris would argue and keep going till the end of days just to prove a point, but he was happy she saw reason, for once.

He had his lashes slightly lifted, not enough for her to notice, and he saw when she turned her attention to him. Iris might think him oblivious to the way her energy shifted every time he had her full attention, and he wanted to keep it that way.

Something bigger was at play and Fern was adamant that he'd discover it before he let her, or her magic, trap him in their clutches. He would be damned if he let anyone have a hold on his life ever again. That lesson had been learned the hard way thanks to that insane king. Be that as it may, he still couldn't help the feelings Iris invoked at the center of his chest or the way his cock hardened every time his focus landed on her. It was almost like the gods were tempting him so they could finally consume his soul. Grinding his teeth, he looked away from her ignoring the pull Iris had on him.

'She is an abomination. Who knows what her magic does and if it's not only a trap for fools like me. Think with your head, not your cock!'

"Here, try this." Darion's voice snapped him from the torrent of thoughts that were making his anger mount. When he opened his eyes, however, he realized his friend spoke to Iris, not him.

"What is the potato-like thingy?" lifting herself up from her reclining position, Iris eyed the fruit in Darion's hand warily.

"It's fruit, you haven't eaten anything, and you'll need your strength." He waved the life star fruit in her face. "Take it."

"Where did you even get this?" Tentatively reaching her hand as if the fruit would bite her, she took it between her fingers. "I thought everything was dead around here." Turning it between her fingers, her gaze lifted to Darion's face. "Could it be poisonous to humans?" Her question made Darion frown, and his hand raised as if debating taking it back.

"You're not human!" Fern winced at how harsh his words sounded but kept his face stoic.

"You don't say, elf." Iris glared at him, her green eyes sparkling with anger. Darion only slapped his hand over his face as if the sight of Fern pained him.

Iris fumed at Fern's audacity, the mixed signals he gave her and most of all, at the anger coming off him like waves that she didn't deserve. This was why she stayed away from people and kept to herself. If she didn't care about what they thought of her or how they saw her, she would not feel this ripping pain in her chest. Unshed tears burned, but she would be damned if she let the jerk see how much his words hurt her.

To add insult to injury, those stupid symbols on her hip started pulsing. She scrunched up her face, breathing, deeply hoping to stop the buildup of magic in her chest.

'You are stronger than this. You can control it.' She kept chanting in her head until the pressure faded, and she sagged in relief.

When she finally looked around her again, she found

Darion watching her with curiosity and something like awe on his face. Fern eyes, on the other hand, were narrowed with suspicion. 'What's new?' she thought angrily.

"What?" Ignoring the jerk, Iris raised an eyebrow at Darion.

"What were you doing?" At her confused expression, he waved his large palm indicating her entire body. "You glowed a little." Tilting his head left and right, making his long hair slide over his bare shoulders he frowned slightly. "Similar to the glow Ivy has... but not really. It was not golden."

"It was not light either." At Fern's comment, she looked sharply at him, and fear squeezed her throat making speech impossible.

"It was beautiful!" Darion snapped glaring at the other Fae while his citrine eyes glowed. Iris smiled sadly at Darion in gratitude.

Whatever she was about to say stayed lodged in her throat as the energy around them shifted. The warmth from the hot weather evaporated making her shiver, and goosebumps covered her from head to toe. Darion and Fern, picking up on her stiffening body, went on full alert.

Fern didn't move, not wanting to alert whoever it was that they were aware of them. He scanned the area around them looking for anything out of place. Darion shifted subtly and stood crouched in front of Iris as if expecting her to climb on his back. All three of them were prepared to move the second they saw who, or what, was nearby watching them. Cold sweat trickled down Iris's spine.

Iris almost jumped out of her skin when a warm, callused palm settled over her hand that was subconsciously squeezing the life out of her cloak. Her head tilted down, and she followed up the arm until they connected with

Fern's blue, glowing gaze. Fern moved his head barely perceptively tilting his chin to indicate she should climb on Darion's back. In the middle of the situation they were in, Iris couldn't find the strength to slap his handsome face.

"I'm not a monkey!" she squeezed the words through clenched teeth and snatched her hand from underneath his.

"We need to move fast, get on his back!" Fern snapped under his breath. This time Iris lifted her hand and fast as lighting slapped him.

The slap echoed in the silence like a bullet fired from a gun at a close range. Both Iris and Fern froze, Iris in shock as she watched the red palm print appear on his face and Fern at her audacity to do such a thing.

Without looking behind, Darion snorted then coughed something between choking and a quiet laugh. Fern's lips parted, no doubt to yell at her or say some other mean words.

The ground underneath them shook, a moment before it split open a few feet in front of Darion. A shadow just like the one Iris fought with Artemis and Ivy flew out and released a screech so loud that all three barely stayed conscious. When the cry stopped, the white glow of the shadow's focus homed in on Iris. Her heart stopped as if wishing to die before that thing got its claws into her.

Chapter Thirteen

Before Iris could protest or even notice that he'd moved, Fern wrapped his hands around her waist and flung her onto Darion's back. On instinct, her legs wrapped around him and she grabbed hold of his shoulders to stop herself dropping to the ground. Fast as lightning, Darion twisted around and bolted in the opposite direction to the shadow with Fern hot on his heels. Iris never would've assumed that the Fae were this fast. It might've been the adrenalin rushing through her veins, or the horror of seeing another shadow, but she was confident the Fae were even quicker than the vampires.

The wind stung her face, her hair streamed behind her pelting her skin. She clutched Darion harder, her nails digging dents in his skin. If it bothered him, he didn't show it. Holding one of his short, wicked swords in one hand in a white-knuckled grip, he wrapped under her thigh holding her to him.

In the middle of it all, Iris couldn't stop the ping in her chest that it wasn't Fern carrying her, but he'd chosen to throw her on Darion. She shouldn't care, but she did. That was until she twisted to look over her shoulder and saw Fern guarding their back with a long staff with glowing symbols on it. Where he pulled that staff from was an enigma but Iris was starting to get used to not having all the answers around the Fae. Fern ran while swinging the staff around his body in wide arcs, the light blue glow of the symbols creating beautiful shapes of circles and infinity symbols around him. It kept the shadow away from them, although it didn't stop its pursuit.

As Iris watched him mesmerized, guilt at thinking ill of him ate at her. Fern looked like some fantasy character in a book. His beautiful face was set in determination, his full lips pressed in a thin line and a slight frown pulled his eyebrows over his intense glowing blue gaze. His silky black hair flew behind him, the speed of their running making the strands flip and twist in the air. His bare torso glistened, the muscles jumping and twitching with the movements of his arms, and his abs stood out, clenched in anticipation. She looked at him greedily without shame while her heart beat faster at the beauty and power radiating from him. The running caused his black pants to drop lower on his hips emphasizing the V lines dipping in the waistband. Subconsciously her legs tightened around Darion, and misunderstanding her, he gripped her harder under her thigh.

Fern's focus zeroed in on the movement, and his jaw clenched harder making a muscle jump like a heartbeat on the side of his face. His swinging faltered. Over his shoulder, Iris saw the second the shadow noticed the opening and added more speed heading for Fern with its mouth open, razor-sharp white teeth glinting in the light. Without thinking she cocked her free arm that wasn't gripping Darion's shoulder.

The First Secret

Fern wasn't sure what happened. One second all his focus was on swinging his weapon and making sure the shadow kept its distance. The next, Darion pulled Iris closer to his back and red bathed everything around Fern. Darion had no right touching the witch, and he ignored the fact that he'd put her on Darion's back in the first place. Jealousy reared its ugly head, and he almost swung his staff at Darion's head. That thought evaporated when a strange light enveloped Iris a second before she lifted her arm looking straight at him. On instinct, he ducked out of the way. The air stirring next to his ear as the fruit went sailing past his head.

A shriek sounded, and the shadow fell behind. Looking over his shoulder, without slowing down he saw the gray shadow writhe around the fruit like smoke coiling up in the air. Whatever the reason, it slowed the thing down, so he pushed harder to catch up to Darion. Fern didn't miss the look of shock on Iris's face as she stared with her lips parted at the shadow.

"We can lose it at the hills," Fern called, putting power in his voice just enough so that Darion could hear him through the whistling of the wind. "We can split up; I'll try to lure it in the opposite direction. You make sure she stays safe!" Darion nodded once sharply not even looking at Fern.

"I can look after myself, thank you very much. You make sure your ass is safe, elf!" Iris yelled. Darion staggered slightly before catching himself. His booming laughter echoed around them making the shadow screech from a distance.

"Try not to strangle her until I get back. She doesn't have control over her mouth." Glaring over his shoulder Fern whirred off to the left not missing a beat.

"I saved your stupid ass, elf! With a potato fruit!" Iris yelled after him. "You're welcome!"

It looked to her like Fern ran faster at her words, but she could've imagined it. Darion tilted to the right and headed in the opposite direction. Iris couldn't help twisting around to see where Fern was going, and worry gnawed at her that the shadow would go after him while he was on his own. Her heart skipped a beat when she saw the glowing patterns of his weapon in the distance and the shadow following behind him.

"We should go after him," Iris yelled at Darion, but he didn't slow down or acknowledge her. He kept running, putting more distance between her and Fern.

Annoyed that Darion would listen to Fern but ignore her, Iris poked him as hard as she could with her finger on his shoulder, repeatedly.

"Hello! I said we should go after him! I'm not sure he can fight the shadow on his own." Her throat hurt from screaming the words, but she didn't care. Fern was on his own with that creepy thing, and fear for his life made her irrational.

"Fern will live. He always does, Iris." Darion's voice sounded like it came through a speaker, making her wince and almost lose her grip on his shoulders.

"Have you seen anything like that shadow before? How can you be so sure?" Her question made Darion glance over his shoulder, his citrine eyes flashing for a second.

"No, I have not, but he is one of the best warriors we have after Artemis. He will be fine."

"You are as stupid as he is!" Pissed off, Iris released his shoulders and wrapped both her hands in his long black hair. Arching her back, she pulled on it as if she was trying to rein in a horse. She didn't release him until he staggered and then stopped, grunting in pain.

"Human!" Panting slightly, Darion glared daggers at Iris, and she beamed at him proudly like a two-year-old.

"So now I'm human? What happened to Iris?"

"I could've dropped you, damn it! At that speed you could've broken your neck!" Fuming, he clenched his fists so hard Iris heard the bones cracking.

"But I didn't!" Snapping back, she fought the shiver that passed up her spine at the thought of dying here from a stupid fall while a ton of people and creatures were trying to kill her. "You don't understand, we must go after him, Darion." She implored him silently hoping that he wasn't as bullheaded as Fern. "Even Artemis couldn't fight the shadow off. I had the protection of magic around us when Ivy somehow got to it, but it cost her a lot. Artemis couldn't do anything. And now we've sent Fern on a suicide mission."

"This is the same shadow?" frowning Darion cast worried glances toward the horizon.

"Ivy destroyed that one, but this one is exactly the same." Reaching, Iris grabbed hold of his hand clinging to it in desperation. "Please, Darion. If we don't go now, we might be too late!"

"If you are wrong, he will have my head, friend or not." He glared at Iris, but she could tell doubt and worry had taken hold of him.

"And if I'm right, he will be grateful. And alive!" Tugging on his hand, Iris walked backward. "If nothing else, at least my magic can keep us safe for a while until we have a solid plan." What she didn't tell him was that it'd hurt like a bitch all the time she held the protection. 'He doesn't need to know that as long as we can protect Fern,' her mind supplied.

"Hop on, and don't you dare pull on my hair like that, ever again." Bending his knees, his look sent dire warning of retaliation if she pulled that on him again.

Iris blushed all the way to the roots of her hair. She couldn't believe that she'd actually reined him in like a runaway horse.

"Sorry," mumbling, she shuffled towards him. "I freaked out a little thinking of what could happen to him." She tried to reach for his shoulders, but a sharp pain in her hip made her stagger. 'Oh hell, no. Not again!' she screamed in her mind.

"You are forgiven." Darion's face softened, and oblivious to her pain, he turned again so she could climb on his back.

Iris knew that it'd be unbearable, and she might pass out while he ran, but she couldn't waste more time. Every second she stood here it could cost Fern his life. Grinding her teeth so hard she thought her jaw would break, she grabbed Darion's shoulders and wrapped her legs around his hips.

"Don't worry, Iris." Misunderstanding her grimace and the tight grip she had on him, Darion petted her thigh. "We will find him before you blink."

With that, he bolted like an arrow again, and Iris prayed with everything in her that he was right. Because if it took longer than a few minutes, she wasn't sure she would be conscious to help when they did find him.

Chapter Fourteen

As Darion raced in the direction that Fern had taken, Iris held on with all the strength in her. The pain had dulled a little, so she was able to at least breathe through it and stay conscious. It still felt like someone had stuck a hot poker in her side and was twisting it slowly. Dark spots danced in front of her, so she tried to look around them to distract herself.

For the first time, she noticed the faint outlines of hills in the distance and a mixture of excitement and dread swirled in her stomach. Iris pressed her face into his shoulder because it felt like Darion had kicked up a gear. Maybe finally her words penetrated his brain, and he understood the danger of Fern's situation. However, the only thing Iris could concentrate on at the moment was that with each second the pain lessened.

Fern raced towards the distant hills doing his best not to think about Iris, or specifically about Iris alone with Darion while she was wrapped around him. He knew how ridiculous he was acting but the witch pushed all his buttons just by her mere existence, and there was nothing he could do about it.

Not even Ivy knew what Iris was capable off and that thought set Fern on edge. It reminded him too much of Lazarus, and everything in him rebelled against the idea of anyone having that much control over him.

The screech of the shadow behind him made his anger bubble up, and he pushed harder to get to the rocky hills so he could take it out on the creature. Fern never considered himself cruel, but the internal war in him tore at his sanity. He wanted to lose himself in Iris, but at the same time he feared that she might be like Lazarus and he wanted wrap his hands around her neck so she couldn't hurt him or anyone else.. Swirling his staff around him, making sure the shadow kept its distance he ground his teeth together and pushed all thoughts out of his mind.

The ground changed from dirt and dried up soil, to a pebbled rocky path. In less than a few blinks, he bent his knees pushed off the ground as hard as he could and sailed up in the air towards the sharp edges of the rock in front of him.

Darion held Iris so tightly around her thighs that his arms were going numb. He wasn't sure if it was because he wanted to make sure she didn't fall, or because her words echoed in his head that Fern might die. Lately, his friend had been an ass, but Darion cared about him like a brother. Fern had the superior strength and shouldn't be underestimated, but Darion had speed on his side. That might help when Fern saw him, he would hopefully know that reaching him had more to do with innate speed rather than Darion's desperation to find him while he still breathed.

When Iris spoke to him, her eyes almost glowed like a Fae's, and some ancient power that made shivers rake his

The First Secret

frame looked back at him through her. Darion wasn't sure what exactly was going on with her, but he knew two things. Fern cared a lot about her even though he fought it, and Artemis would have his head if anything happened to Iris. With that in mind, it could be the devil himself looking at him through Iris, but he would protect her with his life. 'If I reach Fern in time, I might actually keep my life after all this is over,' Darion thought glumly and put more speed.

Fern cursed his broad shoulders when he got stuck between two sharp rocks in his attempt to hide. He stupidly ran straight for the tiny gap, looking at what was past it. The caves were staring him in the face and he didn't use his brain when he should've. He knew that when he found the right cave entrance nothing will follow him there. So, instead of taking the longer time to go around them, or even climb, he literally gave his life on a platter to the damn thing. The shadow had proved to be more intelligent than he'd initially thought. Every time he managed to find a small opening or an entrance to the many caves in these hills the shadow would follow shortly after like a hound dog sniffing for its prey.

Grinding his teeth, he jerked his shoulders sideways scraping his skin in the process and instead of sideways, he was now stuck with his back exposed to the creature. He couldn't have made for an easier pray. He was a sitting duck, and the damn thing was never far behind him. No matter how hard he pushed, it felt like the rocks were moving closer trapping him between them with his arms pinned to the sides.

"How in the worlds did I get stuck like this," he whispered through clenched teeth, still wiggling to free himself.

Fern stilled when the air around him shifted, and the hairs on the back of his neck stood on end. He stopped struggling, holding his breath in hopes that by some miracle the shadow would pass by; otherwise, he was screwed. Standing as still as a statue and clenching his jaw, he did his best not to flinch when a feeling like icy fingers trailed up his spine. The air around him dropped in temperature and his skin pebbled at the drastic drop. His knuckles turned white with the strength of his grip on his staff, but he didn't move. The shadow was right behind him. Fern could feel its icy putrid breath on his skin and the ghostly feeling of its shadow form pressing closer. At that moment his heart beat so fast, it felt like it wanted to escape without him.

He miscalculated the strength of the shadow, and it was too late to turn the situation in his favor. Fern felt his life force slowly leaving his body, and he became weaker by the second.

Out of nowhere, green smiling eyes popped in his mind so vivid that it took Fern a second to realize that Iris was not standing in front of him, but she was in him, in his heart and soul. The thought of Iris flipped a switch inside him. His heart slowed to a regular beat, his whole body relaxed, muscles unclenched, and calmness enveloped him like a blanket. He would die at any moment, but she would live. If his life were needed for her to be safe, he would give it willingly. He stopped struggling against the shadow. If what Ivy said was true, Iris would heal his realm, and everyone would be safe. He'd done his duty, and he'd protected her to the best of his ability. She would live.

A lump clogged his throat at the thought of never seeing her again. At death's door, he sifted through his feelings, with no judgment or restraint. What he found took his breath away. He was angry at himself for not being able to protect her better when Claude came after them. He was mad at himself for letting Lazarus drag him by the nose in circles until it was too late. And he'd taken it all out on her, blaming her for things she had nothing to do with because he'd been scared that he wasn't good enough for her. Fear had gnawed his insides that if he allowed her to get close to him, she would find him lacking.

A puff of icy air exited his lungs and clouding his face as all the weight pressing on his chest lifted when he had no other option but to face himself. In the end, he was just a coward. Scared of a witch who barely reached his shoulder. He felt his energy slowly draining from him, and his legs gave out causing him to almost dangle between the two rocks still holding him prisoner. Her face still floating behind his closed eyelids, and a small smile lifted the corners of his mouth. The cold was taking over his body, and he wasn't sure if it was a memory of her or a hallucination. Whatever it was, he was grateful to see her one last time before he died.

"Oh, Iris." With a heavy sigh, he whispered her name. "I wish I had more time."

"If you stop playing the sleeping beauty, we can get the hell out of here. You'll have plenty of time then."

Chapter Fifteen

At first, Fern thought he imagined Iris's voice and his heart clenched at the sound of it. That was until the shriek of the shadow nearly burst his eardrums, and the cold that froze his insides retreated leaving him feeling like a thawed piece of meat between the two rocks. It was gone and replaced by the warm air as fast as it arrived.

"Fern." Darion's deep voice made Fern look around confused, and he wiggled weakly to see where it was coming from.

"Darion, I think he is stuck... or hurt." The worry in Iris's voice made him warm up inside a lot faster.

"I'm fine," he mumbled barely above whisper not wanting her to see him as pathetic as he felt at the moment.

"I'm sorry about this." That was all the warning Darion gave before his large hand shoved between his shoulder blades, and he was propelled forward, dropping on his hands and knees.

"Oh my god, he's bleeding." Looking at the blood

covering Fern's arms Iris was horrified. In her head, he was bleeding to death, and she felt faint at the sight.

"He'll live, Iris. It's nothing but scrapes from the rocks." Darion couldn't hide the amusement in his voice. "We need to get out of here before that thing comes back."

Finally, Fern was able to take a deep breath, and he turned around to see where the other two were. Darion stood almost on top of him, looking down as if expecting him to argue, but Fern couldn't be bothered with his friend at the moment. His focus stayed on the woman who stood protectively in front of them, palms lifted in the air in front of her pushing a shimmering purple shield towards the snarling, snapping shadow that threw itself at it. Such a tiny little creature, but she had so much fire in her that she took Fern's breath away.

"Do you need help to get up, or are you going to gape at her all day?" Darion waved his palm in Fern's face.

"I thought I told you to keep her away from the shadow." Taking the offered hand, Fern lifted himself up grunting from the needle-like sensations assaulting his entire body.

"Have you tried making her do something that she doesn't feel like doing?" Darion grabbed his arm to steady him as Fern swayed on his feet. "How did that go for you?"

"Ladies, we need to go." The strain in Iris's voice made Fern snap to attention at once." You can exchange beauty tips later. I'm not sure how much longer I can hold it away."

Snatching his staff off the ground Fern was next to her in two long strides. Darion came to flank her on the other side as the three of them faced the writhing shadow. Iris had never felt such joy as when she saw Fern standing next to her.

When she and Darion finally found him, she thought

she would die from a heart attack. Fern was sandwiched between two large boulders, and the creepy shadow was wrapped around him like a lover, the mouth full of sharp teeth close to his neck. Everything around them was frozen like some macabre ice castle, the ice sparkled in rainbow colors. Fern's frozen hair sat around his shoulders like a diamond helmet and everything in Iris screamed that she was too late. He wasn't moving, wasn't fighting, he just stood there still an ice sculpture.

Darion dropped her on the ground and threw himself at the shadow, but the damn thing only snarled him in its icy embrace as well. That snapped Iris out of her shock and pain, and her palms shot up in the air sending a blast of purple energy at the shadow. It shrieked as if she'd ripped its heart with her bare hands and bolted away from the two men. That was enough for Iris to run and place herself as a guard between them and the shadow.

Grinding her teeth, she tried her best not to show how painful it was to hold the shield up. Again, like the last time, she couldn't pull her hands down or break the connection with her magic. Unfortunately, Fern was as perceptive of some things, as he was oblivious of others.

"You can lower the protection now, Iris. I will hold it back." Fern twirled his staff away from her as if trying to show her that he really could do what he claimed.

"I can't." Her voice was more breathless then she liked, but the pain and Fern's nearness together were making her ready to faint.

"Of course, you can. I'm not injured, I'll hold it back." Frowning slightly at her lack of faith in him he tried to pull her behind him, but she dug her heels not moving an inch.

"Iris…" There was a warning in Fern's voice, but Darion grabbed his arm in a tight grip shutting him up.

The First Secret

"She's not saying she doesn't want to, you fool." Glaring at his friend Darion jerked him away from Iris. "She is saying she can't. Look at her arms."

That's when Fern noticed her struggling with her own body. Her shoulders were hunched slightly like she was trying to pull the shield towards her, but her arms stayed up in front of her as if they were not part of her body. Fear grabbed hold of Fern's heart, and he dropped his staff before pushing Darion away, making him stagger back a few steps. Stepping around her, Fern placed both hands on her face. His gut dropped at the pain on her face and the unshed tears glistening on her long eyelashes.

"Iris, how do I stop this?" He searched her face, but she only stared back at him unblinking. "Please," his voice broke, and he had to clear his throat. "Please tell me how to stop it."

"I don't know how." Iris pushed the words through numb lips.

The worry in Fern's eyes made her heart beat faster. So, he didn't really hate her like she assumed. It made the pain a lot more bearable. He kept holding her face between his warm palms and stood there as if by sheer of will alone he would make the pain go away. Her heart melted even more, then swayed a little when the shadow hit the shield again and drained her a bit more.

Darion, in his fear that something would happen to Iris, took hold of her arm and yanked as hard as he could, hoping to lower it.

To Iris, it felt like he was trying to pull her arm out of its socket and a scream ripped out of her throat before she could stop it. Before she could react, Fern's fist connected with Darion's face sending the other Fae flying back, until his back hit the side of the rocky hill and his head smacked off it before he dropped to the ground. Moving around her again he started going after Darion with a feral growl rumbling in his chest.

"Fern, please!" Iris called out making him turn towards her. "He was trying to help. Please don't hurt him."

Groaning Darion lifted himself to his feet and wiped the blood dripping from his split lip with the back of his hand. His citrine eyes were not glaring at Fern. They shone like he was fighting tears and they were trained on her. Iris gave him a weak smile in hopes of showing him that this wasn't his fault. It only made him hang his head in defeat, his black hair falling like a curtain hiding his face.

"Fern, please," Iris repeated looking back at the furious Fae in front of her. "Is there somewhere we can go without this thing following?"

"The caves are the only thing I can think of. That's where I was headed." The glow in his gaze faded slightly, and Fern stepped closer to her again.

"Then let's go!" Determination set on her face as Iris straightened her shoulders. "I'll walk backward, you guide me, so I don't break my neck."

Without saying a word Fern stepped so close to her she could feel the heat of his body on her skin. Ducking around her, he popped up a breath away from her face between her outstretched arms and grabbing her waist, he lifted her up. Iris wrapped her legs instinctively around him and regretted it the next second. As soon as her core connected with his bare lower stomach, electrical current zapped through her, sending her mind spinning and hormones raging.

Fern's nostrils flared, and his eyes glowed a deeper shade of sapphire as he looked at her with so much hunger that the breath froze in her lungs. And then, as if loving torturing her, his hands grabbed hold of her ass and pressed her closer to him.

Iris forgot all about the shadow, the magic draining the life out of her, and the pain. At that moment, all she knew, all she saw, was Fern. The clearing of a throat brought all the unpleasant sensation back, and she broke the eye contact looking down at Fern's chest as it moved up and down a lot faster than usual with each breath he took.

"There is an entrance not far from here. Will you be able to go inside while holding the shield, Iris?" Darion's voice helped Iris to snap out of the trance Fern had produced.

"We need to get there, and we will see. I don't fight creepy thingies on regular bases, so I don't have much experience with the shield. It kinda happens when my life is in danger." To distract herself more she tried making a joke as she turned to look at Darion. "It's like pulling a rabbit out of your ass."

"Humans do that?" The horrified look on his face made her snort then almost choke on her own tongue.

"No." She gasped for air before groaning in pain. "It was supposed to be a joke." Fern side-stepped Darion.

"You really are a strange human, Iris." Shaking his head, Darion followed close behind staying far enough from the magic swirling behind them.

"She is not human." Fern murmured close to her ear, but the disgust that usually followed that statement was surprisingly missing in his voice.

Chapter Sixteen

The shadow followed behind them, slamming its ever-shifting body into the shield Iris held up with the last of her strength. Fern and Darion moved as fast as the rocky terrain would allow, skipping over tall boulders like mountain goats. The thought made Iris giggle weakly, the pain making her delirious, but feeling Fern's heartbeat on her chest as she pressed against him told her that even if she didn't make it, it was still worth it.

"She is fading fast, hurry." Darion's voice came through a fog, and her eyesight blurred as she struggled to keep her head up. Fern tightened his arms around her and moved faster, tottering left and right in his need to get to the entrance of the cave.

Iris felt like she was floating in a pool of acid, her skin burning, the pain slowly eating its way from inside. She'd lost the feeling in her arms a while ago which in a way was a mercy because she didn't think she could handle the burning pain from where her magic streamed from her palms. The shield never wavered, nor lost its strength despite her dwindling energy.

Pressing her face into the crook of Fern's neck, she inhaled deeply, filling her nostrils with the scent that managed to make butterflies tickle her belly even though the pain. She'd reached him in time, and he lived. 'That must count for something' she thought to herself. 'He might forgive me for placing his life in danger when I was looking after him.' That thought made her sigh deeply before her world turned black.

Fern's heart stopped, then kicked into high gear when Iris went limp in his arms. The entrance of the caves loomed in front of them like a gaping black hole bringing dread to his stomach. He could feel her heart beat faintly and not as regularly as he would've liked. Darion was yelling, but Fern's mind was blank with only one thought screaming loud and clear in his head, get inside the cave. He didn't even turn around to look over his shoulder to see if the shield was still up as he put a burst of speed and almost went head first into the entrance followed closely by Darion.

The fading purple glow told him that the shield held until they entered the cave, but after a moment it blinked out. The darkness that enveloped them made him stop as if he'd grown roots. Clutching Iris to his chest, he felt Darion pressed back to back with him, as they both panted.

Fern's eyes started glowing casting a faint light across the tunnel bouncing off the smooth walls as he turned his head left and right. He wasn't sure what he was looking for, but better that than thinking about the woman in his arms not waking up only because she tried to save his useless hide.

Sharp pain in his chest made him look down fully

expecting to see an arrow sticking out from it, but only Iris's pale face greeted him making that pain double.

"It's not following into the caves." Darion panted behind him, and Fern finally looked over his shoulder with confusion on his face. "The shadow," Darion spoke in the darkness, only his citrine eyes visible as they glowed faintly. "It's not entering the caves. I can hear it outside, but it's not moving towards us."

"We need to find a place so we can help Iris." With those words, Fern wrapped one arm tightly around Iris and placed the palm of the other on the wall of the tunnel.

"I'm sure there are open areas somewhere where we can stop for a while." Shuffling behind Fern, Darion hopped with everything in him that he spoke the truth.

"Why did you come after me?" After dragging his feet for a while to make sure there were no holes on the ground, Fern growled in annoyance.

"She said that not even Artemis could fight the shadow that attacked them. She was anxious about you, and I must say I'm glad that I listened. Although if she doesn't wake up, I'm not sure how I'll feel about it." The sadness in Darion's voice bounced off the walls creating tiny echoes.

"If she doesn't wake up you won't feel anything because I'll kill you." Rage bubbled up in Fern's chest at the thought. "Ivy thinks that Iris can heal the realm, save all of us, and you thought that my life was more important than hers?" Venom dripped in his voice.

"If I didn't bring her to you, she would've followed anyway," Darion spoke softly as if talking to himself. "Why are you being an ass to her?"

"What?" Taken back, Fern glared over his shoulder in what he hoped was the direction of Darion's face.

"I see the way you look at her when she's not watching.

The First Secret

Yet, when she talks to you, or even when she doesn't, you make comments that make me want to slap some sense into you. I truly don't know how she hasn't done it by now."

"That's none of your business."

"I kinda like her. She is honest and kind. That makes it my business."

"Tread very carefully Darion, we've been friends for too long, but that won't stop me from breaking your neck." Still gliding slowly through the tunnel, Fern scolded him in the darkness. "We don't know what she is. Do you want another Lazarus on our hands?" But even as he said the words Fern knew that they didn't carry the same weight as before.

"You must've lost your mind somewhere in the human realm if you can compare the woman who may die just because she tried to save your ass, with Lazarus." Darion whistled slowly. "You are truly dumber than a rock."

"Shut up!" Fern snapped, angry because he knew Darion told the truth.

"Or what?" Now Darion sounded angry as well. "You're going to break my neck? Go ahead then, break it. It'll still leave you being a dumbass."

"You are itching for a fight. Running didn't do the trick for releasing some pent-up energy?"

"I wouldn't mind actually punching you in that scrunched up face. I don't need to see you to know you are glaring at me."

"What's it to you how I am around Iris?" Fern shook his head, all anger draining out of him. "I thought you liked her, yourself."

"Yeah, but she doesn't want me. You are as blind as you are dumb if you haven't seen the way she looks at you."

"You can stop the insults," Fern snapped, but there was no bite in his words.

"Why, when it's so much fun? The truth is a bitch to hear, isn't it?"

"You have no idea…" Fern whispered on an exhale, pulling Iris closer to him.

"Is that a light?"

At Darion's question, Fern looked up and saw a faint blue glow in the distance. Without another word, he moved faster. As soon as they had some light, he could see what he could do to help Iris.

Chapter Seventeen

As they walked closer to the blue glow, the tunnel become more visible. Fern sped up, taking longer strides and Darion followed. Since they'd noticed the light, Darion hadn't said a word and Fern had remained silent too. Guilt ate at his gut like acid, but he pushed it deep down. First, he needed to make sure that Iris lived, he could deal with his demons later. How he would help her, he didn't know, but he would damn well try.

The tunnel had a fork leading left towards the light, and another leading to the fates only knew where. Neither Fern, not Darion gave the right tunnel a glance as they stormed in an open cavern to the left.

The blue glow emanated from a small lake nestled on the right side. It reflected off the walls that were sprinkled with what looked like quartz at first glance. Opposite the lake, jutted rocks that resembled a stairway made for giants as they stacked one on top of the other. They almost looked strategically placed so that you could climb all the way to the high ceiling where a deep crack in the rock let fresh air filter through the cavern.

If he weren't holding Iris limp in his arms, Fern would've stopped to admire the beauty surrounding him. As things were, he rushed to the lowest jutting rock placing her gently on top of it. He heard water splashing, and a moment later Darion was next to him handing him a carved bowl filled with the sparkling liquid.

"We don't know if it's safe to use it on her." Fern pushed the bowl away with the back of his hand.

Pressing his fingers on her neck, he waited to feel the pulse of her heart. Faintly, after too long for his liking, it bumped against the skin of his fingers. Darion stood behind him, looking over his shoulder making Fern clench his teeth. His friend acted as if Fern would hurt Iris, which was ridiculous. Grabbing the cloak, Fern pulled it apart exposing her body to check for any injuries. As the fabric parted and her body was revealed Darion took a sharp breath.

"Impossible!" Darion gasped, his mouth too close to Fern's ear for his liking.

"You see the same then?" Fern pushed the words through numb lips as he lifted his hand as if ready to touch her before letting it drop limply next to his body.

Darion didn't answer. Instead, Fern heard the rustling of clothing and his head snapped to look over his shoulder. Darion had stripped from his boots and pants. Butt naked, he was twisting his head to look at his own back, turning in circles like a dog chasing its own tail. If Fern weren't feeling numb, it would've been comical to see.

"What do you think you are doing?" At Fern's incredulous words, Darion stopped and looked at him wide-eyed.

"Am I marked?" Fern's gut clenched at Darion's question, and he turned back to look at the glowing symbols on Iris's body.

"No, you're not."

Gently he pulled down the waistband of the pants she was wearing to see the marks better. They shimmered with a golden glow making it look like they were moving. Fern had heard about mating marks, but he had never seen them before he met Iris. None of them had since the queen died and cursed them all to hell. The ancient symbols wrapped around Iris's hip and the side of her waist blinked and shimmering as if laughing at him.

"Are you?" Darion spoke too close to his ear again, and Fern elbowed him to push him back, but the question stopped his heart for a second.

"No." Looking over his shoulder at Darion, he frowned.

"If I'm not marked, I wonder how she managed to touch me while we ran. From what I know about mating marks it would've been excruciating for her." Talking more to himself then Fern, Darion frowned at the symbols. "Or maybe they were only bullshit stories." He looked at Fern sideways, and his citrine eyes narrowed. "Let me see if you are marked."

Before Fern could move, Darion grabbed the waistband of his pants and pulled down. They got stuck just above his groin the fabric digging painfully into his skin, and he tried to move away. Darion, however, was having none of that. Grabbing Fern's shoulder, he turned him around and staggered back a few steps when the glowing symbols, much smaller than the ones on Iris's body, blinked at him from low on Fern's hip.

"You fucking asshole!" The wild citrine gaze blazed like the sun a second before Darion's fist connected with Fern's chin sending him flying back and hitting the jutting rocks.

"And you didn't tell her!" His voice echoed around the cavern as he roared at Fern.

"I didn't know how to tell her." Fern groaned as he lifted himself off the ground.

"With your mouth. Like the rest of us!" Still seething Darion glared daggers at Fern. "She is right, you know. You are bipolar!"

"You don't even know what that means," Fern snapped.

"Whatever it is, I hope it means you are an asshole! You don't deserve a mate!" Those words hurt more than the punch, and he dropped on his ass putting his head in his hands.

After long moments of silence, Darion pushed again, but the anger in his voice was missing. "Are you going to tell her?"

"That's the last thing she needs to worry about right now." Fern's words came out muffled through his hands.

"That's not for you to decide. If you don't tell her, I will." With those words, he stormed out of the cavern still butt naked.

Fern sat there on the cold, wet stone as the chill seeped through his pants and his mind raced. He'd hidden this information from Iris at first because of her similarity to Lazarus. Then he continued holding his mouth shut because he was scared she would resent him. He even convinced himself that he could ignore it. Now that Darion knew, there was no way to keep it from her. She must hear it from him, and Fern wasn't looking forward to that conversation.

Chapter Eighteen

Voices penetrated the fog in her brain and Iris struggled to wake up. A cool breeze drifted gently over her skin, and she wondered if she was naked. Her whole body hurt, and even shallow breaths threatened to rip her lungs apart. 'I guess that's what my life is right now, only pain' she thought. If it wasn't her magic or the creepy shadows trying to kill her, the vampire king took a turn. If that didn't work, then Fern would say or do something, and her heart would shatter into pieces. Iris groaned, half because of the pain, half as a result of her thoughts.

"Iris?" She recognized Fern's musical deep voice, and her face turned towards him on instinct. "Can you hear me?"

She wanted to reply, but her lips refused to move, and the little effort it took to turn her head used up all the strength she possessed. Fern's fingers traced her cheek and jaw barely touching her, but she felt the contact all the way to her core. 'Did I die?' she wondered, confused. Before she had time to ponder that question, she was gently lifted in the air, and a moment later she felt a firm chest pressed to her side. The scent she would recognize anywhere as Fern filled her nostrils and her body sagged more in his arms.

"You think it might work?" Darion spoke from somewhere behind her as Fern gently rocked her.

"Only one way to find out." There was anger in Fern's voice, and Iris wondered what she had missed while she was out cold.

"I'll go look around to see if I find a clue. Call if you need me, I won't go far." That last part sounded like Darion warning Fern not to do anything stupid. Iris's gut clenched.

Fern didn't answer, and she realized the rocking motions were from him carrying her. Finally, Iris heard the soft whoosh of water nearby. She raked her brain to remember if any of them mentioned water being close by, but she came up empty.

Another groan escaped her when Fern jostled her around removing her cloak, then her boots and pants. Iris felt cold and numb, and at the moment she was grateful for it because she would've blushed all the way to the roots of her hair if that was not the case. Her corset was next, and she heard the sharp intake of breath from Fern when her breasts were freed. And then silence. She couldn't even hear him breathe as if he was holding his breath and his hands gripped her tighter, his fingers biting into her skin.

Iris felt the sluggish beat of her heart grow stronger, and the rhythm sped up further at the heat adiating from Fern's body. It was like someone had cranked up the volume on his body temperature and goosebumps covered her arms and legs.

"You are so beautiful," Fern whispered softly under his

The First Secret

breath, if she weren't so close to him she wouldn't have heard it. It was her turn to hold her breath.

Clearing his throat, Fern moved her again, and Iris heard the swishing of water sounding like Fern was walking through it. 'Is it a river?' Iris thought to herself, but her mind went silent when Fern lowered her body, and the warm water covered her up to her neck. It was soothing, and pinpricks tingled under her skin. Iris groaned again when Fern tilted her head back and glided his fingers through her dark hair getting it wet. It felt like heaven, and she wanted to stay like this forever. No thoughts of what was expected of her, no psycho's out for her blood and no frowning or jerk remarks from Fern.

She felt his skin on hers when he held her to him again. Iris pushed through the fog in her mind, and her breathing sped up along with her heart. It was electric feeling him wrapped around her, skin to skin, and a shiver ran up her spine. Unable to stop it, a soft moan escaped her lips.

"Iris?" Cupping her face in his large palm, Fern turned her face towards his. She could feel his breath on her cheek and lips and struggled harder to open her eyes wanting to see him. "Open your eyes, Iris. Show me that you are getting better, please."

Iris pushed with everything in her, and her lashes fluttered before she was able to slightly lift her eyelids. They weighed a ton and felt like they were glued closed. She expected the light to burn or even to see a dark, dingy cave. What Iris never expected, was to see Fern's handsome face and glowing blue eyes staring down at her surrounded by sparking rainbow lights making it look like they were suspended in the sky amongst a million stars.

Relief was written all over his face, and he took a deep

breath lifting his face up as if thanking whatever gods he believed in, that she lived. Iris swallowed thickly at the sight in front of her, and with a lot of effort, she lifted her hand and placed it on his cheek. Painfully slow he tilted his chin down and looked at her again.

"I'll start thinking you were worried about me, elf." Her voice was raspy, and her throat hurt.

"Don't you ever," Fern looked at her in such a way that her chest tightened at the intensity on his face. "do that again, Iris!"

"Do what?" she murmured, "Save your ass?" When he glared at her, her lips tilted in a barely there smile. "I can't promise that, elf. Someone must make sure you don't get in trouble, after all. I volunteered as a tribute." She chuckled weakly under her breath at the quote from one of her favorite movies.

"I'm not worth your life, Iris." Fern's words sobered her up, and all attempts to break the tension fled from her mind. "I don't deserve your loyalty. Not after the way I've acted since you met me." Swallowing thickly, Fern took a deep breath. "No one is worth your life. Not even this entire realm."

"What happened while I was unconscious?" She frowned at him. "Did you hit your head?" Sucking a sharp breath in, she looked at him pretending to be shocked. "Did the shadow mess with your brain?"

"Very funny," Fern drawled, pursing his lips.

"You must admit it was a little funny." Iris blinked innocently at him. "I'll have you know I'm a funny person. Hilarious some might say."

Fern didn't answer. His intense blue eyes searched her green ones as if looking for something. The longer he stared at her, the more aware Iris became that the only thing standing between them were her lace panties and Fern's pants. Fern trying to be a gentleman and keeping those on irritated Iris. All she wanted was to rip them off him and wrap her legs around his waist. At that thought, her nipples pebbled, and Fern's attention zeroed on them. Iris trembled in his arms.

Chapter Nineteen

Fern did his best to make sure that Iris was comfortable and healing. He had every intention of holding himself back so he could help her in the little lake.

Darion accidentally discovered that the water had healing properties when he tried to give some to Fern to help Iris. The cuts and bruises on his hands healed instantly after Darion dipped the bowl in the lake scooping the water up. As soon as he noticed, he pushed Fern to take her inside the water.

They'd argued at first, Fern stubbornly refusing to do it fearing a possible bad effect on her. But after a few hours he decided he had nothing to lose, she wasn't waking up anyway, and her pulse was getting fainter.

The water didn't just help her heal enough to wake up, but the longer they stayed in there, Iris's skin glowed and shimmered around her making her look like a vision.

When she spoke to him, and her sass came out loud and clear, Fern knew he won't lose her. She would get better, and he won't go insane. But the energy shifted, and regardless of

The First Secret

his efforts to only do what she needed to get better, he couldn't control himself anymore. When her nipples pebbled, pointing at him as if begging for attention, and Iris looked at him with a hunger that took his breath away, the thin thread Fern held onto snapped.

Fern snatched her out of the water, and holding his hands wrapped around her waist he placed her not too gently on the side of the lake as she stared at him wide-eyed. If he weren't so lost in the haze of the hunger that consumed him, he would've probably stopped to ask if she was okay. But as things were, all he could think, feel, and smell was Iris. Tangling his fingers in the hair at the nape of her neck he pulled her face towards him and crushed his lips to hers.

Iris was so shocked at the intensity coming in waves off Fern that when he tilted her head up and devoured her mouth, it took her a second to respond. When he pushed his tongue inside her mouth and started gliding it over and around hers, a desperate moan, low and primal, broke from her throat. She grabbed his long black hair in both her hands and wrapped her legs around him pulling him as close to her as possible. His hands roamed over her body pressing her firmly to his chest as if he wanted to touch all of her at the same time. Her skin pebbled in the wake of his touch. She arched, rubbing her aching nipples on his firm pecs. Fern growled in her mouth. Iris wasn't sure what she wanted, but whatever it was that they were doing, it was not enough.

"More." The sultry, breathless voice coming out of her mouth surprised her when she pulled away from Fern to take a breath.

Taking advantage, Fern pulled her head back still holding her hair at the nape, and as she arched her back, he latched on, sucking her nipple in his mouth. The sounds coming out of Iris's mouth only spurred him on. She whimpered, mumbled his name, moaned deep and long, as he nipped, licked, and sucked at her breasts like a man possessed.

"I want to be inside you." His voice, deeper, full of lust and hunger made liquid pool at her center.

"Yes...yes...yes..." Iris mumbled, tilting her hips and grinding on the hardness trapped by the wet fabric of his pants.

Fern pulled back and with a large palm pressed between her breasts, pushed her down on the ground. As Iris lay down, his palm traveled down from between her breasts to her belly, until his fingers stopped at her panties. The nude color lace left nothing to the imagination, the water making it almost transparent as it stuck to her folds. A groan made her look from his hand to his face. He was staring at her wet center, the glow of his blue gaze almost pulsing in sync with the throb in her channel. Her entire body trembled with need and Iris was ready to start begging.

Fern trailed his fingers over her hip where the symbols glowed, and Iris thought she was about to orgasm. Her entire body felt like it caught fire and she screamed his name arching her back so high she almost lifted her body off the ground. Fern grabbed hold of her hips keeping her lower body pinned down until she dropped her back and looked up at him heavy-lidded through her lashes.

"Do it again." Her voice rasped, and her tongue poked out to wet her suddenly dry lips. They were both panting, and Iris noticed Fern's hands shook where they held her hips.

"About these symbols..." Fern's voice trailed off, and at her confused look, he stepped away from her.

Iris opened her mouth ready to beg or scream at him to finish what he started, but the words died on her tongue when he untied the laces on his pants and pulled them down his hips. His thick cock popped free pointing towards his belly button Iris had to swallow hard and dig her nails into to ground, to stop herself reaching for it. The man was too good-looking to look at when he was dressed. Naked, he looked like something that should be hidden from the world and worshipped.

She had to try very hard to pull her attention away from his hardness, but finally, with a lot of effort, she looked up at his face. Her channel pulsed, gripping emptiness. She wished he'd just push his cock inside her so deep that she wouldn't know where he ended, and she began.

"Can we talk about those later?" Iris winced at the desperate tone of her voice.

"They are mating marks." Fern sounded as desperate as her, and it took Iris a moment to realize he was pointing at his own hip.

Chapter Twenty

Right next to the V line on Fern's hip, a smaller version of the symbols that Iris had on her hip glowed faintly. It took Iris couple of tries to keep her gaze centered on the symbols instead of drifting back to the cock twitching close to them. As if it could sense her eyes on it, every time she looked, it pulsed while the defined abs above it contracted. It made an answering pulse go through her core.

"Oh look! Matching tattoos!" Still panting, she managed to look at Fern's face while her attempt at humor failed.

"Not tattoos they are mating marks." Fern looked at her unblinking, watching her like a hawk as if even the twitch of single muscle would tell him what he wanted to know. "Marks that have not appeared amongst my people for centuries. We almost started believing they are a tale for younglings."

"So, we are mates? Is that what you are telling me?" At her question Fern blinked once very slowly. "Okay, let me rephrase that. Does having mating marks like mine bother you?" Iris held her breath fully expecting him to say he hated the idea. To her surprise, Fern smiled, and his entire face softened.

"No, Iris. It doesn't bother me at all. This is a blessing beyond anything my people could've hoped for. I am honored you chose me." Those words made her brain screech to a stop, but the cock she couldn't stop glancing at twitched again.

"Is there something we can do about it?" Squirming Iris did her best to keep looking above his shoulders.

"No, I just—"

"Okay, good," she spoke over him. "Now let's finish what we started, and we can talk about the mating symbols thingies later."

"Are you sure?" Fern clenched his fists as if holding himself back from grabbing her. "There is no going back after this."

"Fern," Iris decided she'd had enough, and honesty was the best policy before she turned into a begging, blubbering mess. "If you don't get inside me right now, I might actually die right here in this dingy cave."

She expected him to throw himself at her as intense and crazed as he'd been a moment ago. To her surprise, Fern placed his hands on her face, holding it between them, before trailing them slowly down her neck towards her chest. With all the patience of a saint, his fingers glided over her skin. Gently cupping her breasts and rolling her hard nipples between his fingers, he groaned in sync with Iris and continued his exploring of every dip and curve of her body. When his fingers reached her belly and stopped at the top of her panties, Iris lifted her hips slightly, wordlessly begging him to touch her where she needed him.

"You are such a passionate creature, Iris." Giving in to her demands, Fern cupped her core, the heel of his palm pressing on her button while his fingers made circles at her entrance.

"More." Iris knew she sounded and acted desperate, but she had no control over her body or her reactions. All she knew, ever since Fern kissed her, was him.

Fern removed his hand and the cold air that replaced it made goosebumps cover her arms and legs. Iris opened her mouth to yell at him to stop playing games, but the tearing of fabric left her gaping at his smiling face as he ripped her panties to shreds. She barely had a chance to take a breath before he grabbed her thighs, spreading them wider and pushed his broad shoulders between her legs. Still holding her captive with his gaze, he buried his face in her core, and his tongue worked her expertly.

Iris arched her back almost pushing him away when he ate her like a man dying of thirst in a desert. Unable to maintain eye-contact any longer, she threw her head back and buried both hands in his hair. Holding him between her legs, her hips gyrated riding his face. The sounds he made, something between a groan and a growl, drove her insane.

One of Fern's hands stayed on her thigh, holding it in a bruising grip, while his other hand found its way to her opening. Two thick fingers entered her at once and pressing her heels on Fern's back Iris arched her body so high that only the crown of her head touched the ground. Fern moved with her, not losing his rhythm or the intensity of his sucking, nips, and licks. When he inserted a third finger and gently nipped at her button with his teeth, Iris exploded. Like from a distance, she heard herself screaming Fern's name, but she floated in ecstasy between bursts of colors that she couldn't be sure if the screams were real. After what felt like an eternity, she slowly came down, and she realized that Fern hadn't moved away from her core. He still had his face between her legs, giving her outer lips slow sensual licks and placing soft, gentle kisses on the inside of her thighs.

When Iris fully relaxed from the high of the pleasure, he crawled up her body until his cock nestled between her swollen folds and started gliding through them lubricated from her orgasm. Iris had no strength left to move, so she wrapped her arms around Fern's neck and pressed her face on his shoulder. Pulling his hips back far enough so that the tip of his cock throbbed at her entrance, Fern gave his hips one powerful pump and filled her to the brim in one push. Her walls stretched and pulsed around his wide girth trying to accommodate him but Fern gave her no time to rest. As soon as his hips connected to hers, he pulled back and slammed back in all the way to the root.

"You feel so fucking good," he growled through clenched teeth and started grunting and moaning with each pump of his hips.

Soon the sound of skin slapping skin echoed through the cavern adding to Iris's delirious state. She'd never experienced something this intense in her life. It felt like Fern was entirely inside of her, not only physically with his cock that pumped in and out of her driving her insane. She could also feel him deep within her soul. Like a constant presence that she wasn't aware of until now, his beautiful life essence glowed as it linked with hers. The pressure built in her lower belly again, more intense, more powerful than ever before. Iris wasn't sure she would survive it, the pleasure so intense it bordered pain. 'If my heart stops, what a way to go' she thought in delirium. All she could do was cling to Fern and moan, whimper, and scream. Fern kept going, each thrust of his hips feeling like he was going deeper and deeper inside her.

"Cum for me Iris. Let me feel you milk my cock," Fern growled above her.

Iris kept moaning and calling his name unable to form a sentence if her life depended on it. Then Fern's fingers were tapping on her button at the same time as his sack slapped on her ass. On the third tap, he pressed harder, and Iris screamed his name so loud that her voice cut off in the middle of it unable to hold through. As soon as her inner walls clamped around him and pulsed a mighty roar sounding like her name shook the ground beneath her and she felt warmth bathe her insides as Fern pulsed inside her. It lasted long moments but eventually she relaxed, and her body molded to Fern's. He kissed her neck, his soft full lips feeling cool on her fevered skin. With a faint smile, Iris fell asleep.

Chapter Twenty-One

Shuffling feet woke Fern. He tightened his arms around Iris, pulling her closer and curving his body to hide her from view. Looking over his shoulder, he saw Darion walk into the cavern wearing a gloomy expression.

"What's wrong?" His brain went on full alert, and Iris stirred in his arms.

"Couple of things actually." Without spearing him a glance, Darion walked up to the cloak that was crumpled next to the jutted rock where Fern had placed Iris at first and snatched it off the ground. "One, If I have to listen to you two humping like rabbits often, I might let the shadow kill me." He dropped the cloak next to Fern without looking in their direction. "Cover her please, I'm not dead yet, so a beautiful naked woman will have an effect on me, and I don't want to fight with you right now. We have bigger problems."

Grabbing the cloak, Fern placed it over Iris, and she wrapped it tightly around herself before sitting up and turning to look at Darion with evident humor. Fern shook his head, but his lips twitched at the corners before he managed to hide it from her.

"Thank you, Darion." Iris winced at the soreness in her throat, and a blush crept up over her cheeks. "We were quite loud, huh?"

"You think?" Darion tried glaring at her, but when he saw her awake and talking instead of deathly pale and unconscious, his gaze softened.

Iris giggled before slapping a hand over her mouth.

"I blame it on the elf." She pointed an accusing finger at Fern and Darion laughed at the grimace Fern made at being called an elf.

"What are these bigger problems?" Grabbing his still wet pants, Fern struggled to put them on.

Iris hummed a song under her breath, and her thumb moved to touch the tips of her fingers. Both Darion and Fern stopped and stared at her like she had grown a second head. She ignored them, letting her magic build in her chest. After a moment, she lifted her hand and wiggling her fingers towards Fern's pants. A purple mist sparkled in the air, and the pants were dry in Fern's hands.

"Is that how you always bring out your magic?" Darion asked, awe clear in his voice.

"It's the easiest way." She shrugged her shoulder as if she didn't just manipulate energy.

"That was beautiful." At Darion's sigh, Fern shoved his legs in his pants and jerkily tied them.

"The problems, Darion. Not my mate!" He glared at his friend. A snort escaped Iris, and at his narrowed look she gave him an innocent smile. "It won't work, Iris. There is not one innocent bone in your body, woman!"

"The faction that separated from the hunt because they

still wanted to follow Lazarus's plan are in the caves, too." All the humor fled, and Iris and Fern stiffened at his words.

"Did you see them?" Fern grabbed Iris's hand, pulling her up to stand." Go dress!" He pushed her gently towards her clothing. "How many of them are there? And where exactly are they?"

"A few caverns to the right. There are many of these, just like this one only with no lakes. We were lucky to find this one as soon as we walked into the caves. The damn place is a labyrinth." Placing his hands on his hips, Darion frowned at the ground. "About twenty of them, maybe…"

"Oh my god? Twenty?" Now dressed, Iris joined them where they stood near the lake.

"Don't worry, Iris. Nothing will get to you, I promise." Fern tried to soothe her and reached to pull her into his arms.

"Really, elf!" She smacked his hands away making him frown. "You kept saying yourself that I'm not human. I'm not worried about a bunch of elves. I kept the damn shadow thingy away to save your ass, didn't I? I'll send their assess flying just like I sent him." She jabbed her thumb in Darion's direction making him grin from ear to ear.

"Oh, I think I will enjoy the rest of this journey. Especially now." Throwing his head back, Darion laughed while Fern glared at him.

"We are not elves!" Clenching his jaw, Fern pushed the words through his teeth making Iris grin.

"You sure look it, though." She batted her lashes at him. "Pointy ears and all."

Fern couldn't keep up with his frown, so he gave up and just smiled at her. "I never once thought my life will be easy from the first moment I met you." He chuckled shaking his head.

"Alrighty, ...what's the plan?" Iris shook her hands next to her body like a fighter preparing to throw punches. It made both Darion and Fern laugh.

"We do our own thing and avoid them." A plan formed in Fern's mind. "Since Darion knows where they are, and he said himself the cave is like a labyrinth, we will just go around them."

"Well–" Darion started, but Fern wasn't finished. He had to protect his mate whether she liked it or not.

"Unnecessary risks will not be taken. Ivy told Iris that she would find the first secret here. Maybe they know about it, and they're waiting for us. We will not allow them an opportunity to mess with our mission." Fern sliced the air with his arm as if there was no room for debate.

"Technically, it's my mission." Iris pointed out. "You two are supposed to be guides."

"I... umm..." Darion shifted uncomfortably rubbing his neck with his hand.

"Iris, please! You will be the death of me, woman. I know you are strong and can hold your own but please, let me do what I do best. I will not hide you from life, but please don't put yourself in harm's way if there is no reason for it," Fern pleaded with her. "Why do you think Artemis and Ivy wanted me to go with you?"

"To look pretty?" She lifted both her eyebrows at him before she grinned. "Okay, okay. I'll stop joking. It's just that every time a situation gets intense my mouth spits out whatever comes to my mind regardless of if it makes sense. It's my way of dealing with stress I guess." Fern didn't smile or look away from her. "Fine! I will follow your lead, just don't be a jerk."

"Thank you!" A heavy sigh escaped Fern at her promise, and he felt like a weight has been lifted off his shoulders.

"As I was saying, we will do our best to avoid them and to not be seen."

"A little late for that," Darion murmured, and a chill passed over Iris's spine. Fern's eyes glowed as he glared at Darion. "They kind of saw me lurking in the shadows."

"And you came straight here where my mate is?" Fern yelled and punched him in the face.

Darion stumbled but stayed standing. "As much as that was deserved, I would never lead trouble to you mate, old friend. I lost them through the tunnels before I came back."

Fern felt horrible for acting on his anger and grabbed his hair in both hands looking at Darion. "So, what do we do now?"

"Now we make them sleep." Iris grinned.

Chapter Twenty-Two

On silent feet, they moved through the tunnels. Darion led the way, and Fern took the back so that they had Iris sandwiched between them. She tried to protest, but when they pulled their weapons out of thin air again, she had no argument about who was a better option to take point and rearguard. Her fingers twitched as she did her best not to allow her thumb to move from finger to finger. If her magic built inside her, eventually, it would have to come out. If there was no need for it, she might give away their position.

Darion stopped, and she bumped into his back stumbling back a step. When he looked over his shoulder at her, Iris gave him a sheepish smile. Fern's breath tickled her skin and his hands wrapped around her waist pulling her to his chest.

"I need you to pay attention, little flower. You can get lost in your thoughts later when we are away from danger." Fern's lips touched her ear with his whispered words, and the nickname he gave her turned her into a puddle at his feet.

The First Secret

Iris felt a sappy smile stretch her lips a second before his lips move into a smile on the skin of her ear. Turning her head to look at him, she didn't miss the satisfied smile he tried to cover up with a reassuring nod. She looked at him frustrated before elbowing him so hard he grunted, bending down slightly as the air whooshed out of his lungs.

"You think giving me nicknames will allow you to manipulate me? You ass!" she hissed at him, glaring. "I am paying attention!" Straightening up, Iris lifted her chin and walked away from him jerkily. She passed Darion as well, but he grabbed her arm and pulled her to a stop.

"Iris!" Fern growled, but she turned around placing a finger to her lips and shut him up.

Fern and Darion both went very still, straining to hear any sound to indicate that someone was headed their way. They were so tuned into their other senses that it took them a moment to notice Iris waving a hand to get their attention. When they turned their full attention on her, with a sweet smile, she twirled her hand in the air, flipped them her middle finger and walked into the shadows of the adjacent tunnel.

Closing his eyes, Fern shook his head and huffed a deep breath. Darion chuckled under his breath slapping Fern on his shoulder as he followed behind Iris. Fern took a few more moments to just stare at the ground before slowly walking after them. 'The witch will be the death of me, and I'm immortal.' He chuckled under his breath at that thought.

Slinking through the dark tunnels illuminated faintly with few glowing crystals here and there, trying to avoid the area where the other Fae were waiting was not an easy task. Fern wanted to get them away from that area, but Iris was having none of that. Before they left the safety of the pool cavern, she informed him that she would make sure they didn't need to look over their shoulders the entire time they were in the caves. The air thickened with the stench of wet rock and mud the deeper they went. It was getting warmer too, and their skin soon glistened with beads of sweat, their hair sticking to their skin. All three of them stopped at different times at the sound of a rock falling or the ground under their feet tremble slightly.

Uneasiness built in Iris's chest the longer it took to maneuver around those that meant them harm. She had to take slow steps, fitting her feet between fallen rocks and avoiding puddles in case they were deeper than they seemed.

Unclasping the cloak, she folded it over her left arm, to give her hands something else to do. It wasn't the time to gather her magic yet. And then, she heard it. A low murmur of voices filtering through the air made the hairs on the back of her neck stand on end and her heart speed up. They were getting close, so she pushed her arm back, stopping Fern and Darion from moving. They stood there for a long moment, all three holding their breath trying to decide which way the sounds came from.

Looking over her shoulder, Iris hoped that the two men behind her could see her well enough to read her lips as she mouthed, 'To the left.' In two steps she flattened her back to the wall of the tunnel, creeping up slowly towards the bend at the end so she could poke her head out. Fern and Darion followed suit, but Darion placed his hand on her shoulder to stop her movement and took his place in front. It annoyed Iris that they kept doing it as if they thought she was stupid and would give them away. If anyone knew how to not draw attention, it was her. She'd stayed away from people and blended in the background her entire life.

The First Secret

Stopping when they reached the bend, Darion slowly leaned out checking the way ahead as Fern stopped so close to Iris, she could feel his body heat seep into her bones. Since they'd had sex, her entire existence seemed tuned into him, as if she could tell every twitch of his body no matter his distance from her. It was as distracting as it was exhilarating. Darion snapped his head back to look at them with wide eyes. Some unspoken words pass between him and Fern over her head, and she clenched her fists.

"Stupid elves!" Her words barely passed her lips as she seethed as they acted like she was some clueless little girl. They didn't have time for this, the urgency that something would happen soon pushed Iris to irritation at their overly cautious approach.

She slid down the wall, crouching, with her back pressed to the wet rocks. Ignoring everything around her, she took a deep breath and started humming under her breath. Fern wrapped his fingers around her upper arm, maybe to lift her up, or tell her to shut up, Iris was not sure which. But, when she looked up at him, he froze in place. Iris didn't stop humming even when the low murmur of voices went silent indicating that they'd either heard her or were wondering what was going on. Her voice became louder, the melody passing her lips haunting in its beauty as her soft sultry voice carried and echoed off the tunnels.

Darion and Fern swayed on their feet, and Iris pointed frantically for them to cover their ears, so they don't get affected as much. As soon as they followed her directions, awe replaced their frowns. Iris didn't miss a beat as she continued humming, her thumb moving from the tip of one finger to the next as her magic swirling around her in tune with each note.

Snapping out of his trance, Darion stopped staring at

the human crouched at his feet. Never in his long life has he heard something so beautiful as the sound coming out of her, as she looked as if she attempted to lull herself to sleep. Purple tendrils pulsed around her in time with the song, and they began floating forward passing through the tunnel as if searching for something.

He still felt the effects of her voice, his heart had slowed, and his body felt more sluggish but having his palms pressed firmly to his ears helped a little. If Iris hadn't told them to cover their ears, Darion knew that both he and Fern would've been on the floor sleeping by now.

Fern stumbled slightly passing Iris and Darion as he walked closer to the curve in the tunnel. Carefully he leaned around to look ahead of them. The tunnel continued into the belly of the cave but on the right side few yards away was an opening to another cavern. Light flickered from inside like someone had a fire going, the yellow, orange, and red shades dancing on the gray walls of the opening. Iris's shimmering purple magic pulsed along with it, entering the cavern without the slightest change in direction.

With a frown, he inched around the bend and crept closer careful not to make a sound, so he didn't disturb the melody still echoing around them. His heart thumped in his chest when he reached the entrance and looked inside.

Over thirty warriors were fast asleep wherever they've been standing. The purple mist shimmered around their bodies, cocooning them, while weapons, food, and other items lay dropped carelessly around them. In the vast cavern, not one person stirred. Pulling back his head, Fern hurried back to where Darion and Iris waited.

"You can stop now, Iris." He raised his voice so she could hear him. Her lashes fluttered before lifting to reveal green eyes that took his breath away. They glowed just like

The First Secret

his when he used his power, only hers were green with purple specks through them.

The song cut off and Iris took a deep breath slouching further towards the ground. Fern was next to her before she could see him move, lifting her up and cradling her to his chest.

"I need to see," she told him weakly, and sluggishly waved her arm in the direction of the cavern.

Fern carried her there with Darion close on his heels. When they reached the entrance of the cavern, Darion gave a low whistled as he looked around with interest. Iris did too, trying not to miss any detail in the ample open space.

"I must say, you surprise me more with each passing moment, Iris," Darion mumbled next to her. "I'm thrilled you are on our side; I'll say that much."

Lifting her face to look at Fern, Iris narrowed her eyes at him. "You're welcome, elf." When he frowned, her lips twitched before lifting in a smile. "Not bad for a helpless little flower, huh?"

"Now what?" Darion asked stopping whatever Fern was about to say. Iris wiggled, and Fern let her slide down his body to stand on her own two feet. "How long will they sleep?"

Looking around Iris smiled wider. With confident steps, she walked inside the cavern followed by Fern and Darion. "They'll be out for a while, but just in case—" winking at Fern, she pointed at the coiled ropes sitting to the left next to the wall, "—I say we tie them up."

"You are a lucky man to have a mate like her." Darion's laughter made Iris giggle. Fern tried to keep his frown, but his twitching lips betrayed him, so he laughed too.

Chapter Twenty-Three

It took some maneuvering to make sure everyone was tied up with the rope they had available. Iris stood to the side eyeing Fern as he moved around, muscles bunching while he expertly tied the sleeping Fae to each other. His eyes glowing slightly from time to time as he reinforced the knots with his own ability. Flicking her gaze to Darion, she saw him doing the same.

"They won't wake up anytime soon." She assured them, impatiently shifting from one foot to another. The urgency increased, but she pushed it down the best she could.

"We better make sure we have as much time without dealing with any of them as possible." Not looking away from his task, Fern flexed his arm as he pulled on the rope he held. "Not that I don't trust your power, Iris." Finally looking up, his attention was entirely on her. "I'm not sure I've ever seen anything like it in my life. Not even Lazarus could control so many at once."

"I didn't control them." Iris huffed crossing her arms

The First Secret

over her chest, but she couldn't hide her defensiveness. "I just wanted them to sleep and not give us any trouble."

"What Fern is trying to say," Darion butted in glaring at Fern, "is, that it takes great power to have an effect on so many at once. It's a good thing, Iris." He smiled at her reassuringly. "Fern just hasn't used words for anything other than barking orders in a long time. I'm not sure he remembers how to talk like a normal male."

"I know how to talk!" Fern snapped at Darion, annoyed with him. Darion just lifted both eyebrows as if saying 'you just proved my point' and Iris laughed.

"I think you are right, Darion." She laughed harder when Fern turned his frown on her. "He is just a grumpy old elf." Darion released a deep belly laugh.

"If we are done here, we should go and not waste any more time." Looking around to make sure they hadn't missed anything, Fern pointed towards the entrance of the cavern. "The sooner we find what we are looking for, the faster we can get back to safety."

Darion picked up a few daggers and small weapons, stashing them in little holsters that Iris hadn't noticed before. The man was like a magic bag. He seemed to pull stuff out of thin air without anyone noticing where he's kept them in the first place. Fern noticed her watching and smiled.

"It's one of his gifts." When Iris looked at him in confusion, he jerked his thumb toward Darion. "He can manipulate objects to be smaller so he can fit many in a few small pockets. Darion grinned at her and winked before stuffing another dagger in the same holster as the one before it.

"And what are your gifts, Fern?" Curiosity got the better of her, and she looked at him with an eyebrow raised.

"I feel the energy of objects, that's why I'm a good

tracker. If you need to find something, I can do that faster than anyone else in this realm." Walking up to her, Fern placed his large hand on the small of her back guiding her gently to exit the cavern. The warmth of his hand sent a thrill through Iris, and she had to lock her muscles to suppress the shiver.

"Can you find what we are looking for here?" Iris looked across her shoulder at him.

"No, unfortunately, I need to know what we are looking for to find it." Frowning slightly, he tilted his head in thought making his long hair slide over his shoulder onto his broad chest. Iris tracked the movement of the silky strands; her fingers twitching with the need to touch him and push it back. As if reading her mind, Fern looked down at her, and a wolfish smile stretched his lips.

"You can touch me if you like, little flower. I am your mate, I'm yours to touch."

They walked through the tunnels, Iris lost in her thoughts about what he said, hoping that Fern knew where they were going. Darion kept a few paces behind them, giving them some space to talk. In theory, Iris knew that after everything they'd done, she could touch him if she wanted. She had read enough books to understand what being mates meant in fiction, but those were only make-believe tales about eternal love that every woman dreams about. This, on the other hand, was real life, as crazy as it turned out to be in her case. Eyeing Fern from the corner of her eye she steeled her emotions and decided to ask. If she looked like an idiot, so be it.

"So..." her voice trailed off as she tried to ignore him staring at the side of her face. "Being mates is like what? An uncontrollable need to be with someone, and no one else will do for you? The gods taking your free will to choose and

The First Secret

picking someone for you?" She dared to glance at Fern, but at his horrified expression, she turned to look at him thoroughly.

"No!" Stopping in his tracks, Fern grabbed both her hands in his. "Is that what you think? That I had no say if you would be my mate? Is that why you asked if it bothered me to have the same symbols marking me as yours?" He searched her face. Unable to answer him from the lump in her throat, Iris nodded.

"I'll scout ahead, so you two can talk." Darion squeezed her shoulder as he walked past them and disappeared through the bends of the tunnel.

"Those that have powers—" with a sigh, Fern released one of her hands to rub his face. "—those like me and you, could always mark each other as mates. Until the Queen cursed the portals, and us along with it, it was a normal occurrence. It's the greatest honor to be seen worthy, to be marked. The fates, or gods as you like to call them, don't do it for us, little flower. We make it happen ourselves."

"I sure as hell didn't mark you on purpose. I swear I didn't. I would never do something like that without asking." Now Iris was horrified that Fern would think she'd try to trick him into something.

Throwing his head back Fern laughed, and Iris watched with her lips parted as his beautiful face lit up from the inside. When he looked back at her, his eyes were crinkled at the corners, and his smile stretched his full lips making Iris press her thighs firmly together and squirm.

"Just like humans, we find some people more attractive than others. When you are physically attracted to another like you were to me—" he winked at her his smile growing, and Iris wanted to punch him. "Your power, your magic, tests their power to see if it's compatible. The main reason for mating links is to make both parties stronger. When the link forms and the mating is completed, it's an unbreakable bond. But it's not made if we don't want it. You chose me, as I chose you. Our powers just agreed with our choice. They formed the marks linking us together, making us a strong unbreakable unit."

"That's very strange." Still a little confused, Iris chewed on her lower lip.

"What's strange?"

"I honestly thought you didn't like me." Fern opened his mouth to say something, but she placed a hand over his lips. "You acted like an ass, elf, and you know it! I didn't know what the symbols were. I just assumed they were some crazy manifestation of my magic after I came to this realm."

Kissing the palm of her hand, Fern removed it from his mouth. "I owe you an apology for that, Iris. I hope that one day you will forgive me for acting like an ass. I knew that Lazarus was an evil creature intent on hurting us all. The oath I had no choice but to give almost killed me. Instead of dying, I found myself in two realms at once, my physical body in your realm, my spirit in this one thanks to Ivy. Secrets came out left and right about, Lazarus, the Queen, even about Ivy and her powers. And then when I was finally back in my body... there you were. Your power radiated from you in waves while you kept claiming to be human. Even as a changeling as Artemis assumed, you couldn't be that powerful. I'm ashamed to admit that I feared you more than anything else."

"What changed?" Iris searched his face, holding her breath.

"I was being stupid and acting like an ass, and yet, you still came for me." His gaze shimmered as he watched her face "After everything I said, you didn't think twice before putting your life in danger to save mine. No one has done that for me."

"That's not a good reason, Fern." Pulling her hand away from his, Iris looked away from his face. "I would've done the same for anyone else." Making a grimace, she shrugged her shoulder. "Okay, I wouldn't do it for Claude, but you get my point."

"And that is exactly why, little flower." At Fern's softly spoken words her eyebrows hit her hairline. "You would've done it for almost anyone. There is no evil in you, Iris. You are as far away from Lazarus as day is from night. My fears were just me fighting my own feelings for you. It took both of us almost dying for me to get my head out of my ass, as Darion would say."

"Thank you." Iris smiled tenderly at him. She had trouble accepting compliments, and an even harder time when they came from him. Fern's face darkened, and hunger replaced his apologetic expression. Before Iris realized what was happening, he had her pinned between his firm chest and the rocky wall of the tunnel.

Chapter Twenty-Four

Lowering his head Fern pressed his body harder onto Iris. Her soft curves cushioned his hard body, molding to him like clay. His heart rate picked up, his shallow breathing matched hers, fueling her need for him. Her power pulsed around him, igniting his nerve endings and making him more sensitive than ever before. Even the fabric of her corset and his pants felt painful everywhere they contacted his skin. Burying his nose in her hair, he inhaled deeply, her flowery scent filling his lungs.

"You have no idea what you do to me woman." His deep musical voice made Iris tremble.

"Why don't you tell me." Iris cringed internally at the breathless sound of her voice. She was grateful that Fern had her pressed to the wall because her knees gave out, and she would've been a puddle at his feet if he hadn't been holding her up.

"How about I show you, little flower?" The words rumbled in his chest, reverberating through her body before pooling in her lower belly making her pants wet.

The First Secret

Fern's lips glided gently on her cheek, inching closer to her mouth. Iris slid her hands around his waist and up his back, holding him closer. Everywhere her fingers touched his skin, static made her hands tingle. It all added to the intoxicating feeling Fern invoked whenever he was near.

Iris became acutely aware that she didn't have panties under her pants, the fabric she admired not long ago restricted and scratched her skin. Fern's lips placed a slow openmouthed kiss at the corner of her mouth. A low desperate moan escaped her lips, and her fingers pressed harder into his skin making his growl in return.

"How does this make you feel, little flower?" his words were barely above a whisper, but his heart thundered.

Iris clutched him to her, turning her head, she sought more. She wanted his lips on hers so badly that her body trembled with the force of her desire. Somewhere in the back of her mind, she knew that they didn't have time for this. The sleeping Fae could wake up and come after them, or other dangers could meet them in the caves. All that faded in comparison to Fern's nearness, and what his touch did to her. All the realms could be destroyed, and she'd go along with them wearing a smile if he were holding her like this, and his lips were on her skin.

Fern pulled his head away to look at her when she almost locked her lips on his. His blue eyes blazed as she struggled to hold back, and not grab his hair to pull him back for a kiss. Panting, Iris allowed him to see her desperate need for him.

"I am your mate, Iris. I'm yours to do with as you please." Grinding his hips to her, his hard cock pressed on her lower belly. "Don't hold back on me, little flower. Never hold back on me. Take what you need... please."

It was the please that made something in Iris snap. All

her fears about seeming desperate, or clingy, evaporated with that one word, and the vulnerability Fern bared to her. With a whimper, she pushed up on her tiptoes and kissed him so hard her teeth made the inside of her upper lip bleed. It was all the encouragement Fern needed, and his fingers tangled in her hair while he pushed his tongue inside her mouth. Iris opened for him, clawing at his back, her desire making her animalistic.

One of Fern's hands moved from her hair, down her neck and shoulder until it stopped at the top of her corset. His fingers pushed under the fabric, taking a good hold on it, before jerking it down and freeing her right breast. Without waiting, his hand grabbed the round mound and molded it firmly before his fingers pinched her nipple and rolled it between them.

Iris mewled in desperations which would've embarrassed her if she hadn't been crazed with need. Her hands moved from his back to the firm globes of his ass, and she gripped him as hard as she could pulling him closer while trying to widen her stance. She needed his hardness at her core, but Fern had her still pinned to the wall.

He must've read her mind because he released her lips and moved his body away making her whimper. She wanted to protest, but the air whooshed from her lungs when Fern flipped her around pressing her face and chest to the rocky wall. The skin of her bare breast and the hard nipple scraped on the rock, but the stinging pain only made her desire skyrocket. Her channel pulsed with need, gushing liquid that caused the fabric of her pants to stick to her inner thighs. Fern fumbled with something behind her, but she couldn't turn around to see what he was doing. He held her firmly pressed to the wall with one large palm between her shoulder blades. Iris was about to demand he do some-

The First Secret

thing when he took hold of the waistband of her pants and jerked them down to mid-thigh.

The cold air on her fevered skin didn't have time to register before the hand on her back disappeared, and the next second, she felt Fern's mouth on her lower lips. Taking hold of her hips, he tilted her pelvis back and started eating her from behind like his life depended on it. Iris's mouth opened in a silent scream, and her fingers grabbed hold of the rocky walls to ground herself. If she didn't feel the painful bite of the rock on her fingers, she thought she might float away in a world of lust, and never return.

Fern growled, the sound reverberating in her lower belly and he pushed one thick finger in her channel. Iris pushed back on his face, needing him to do something, anything, to satisfy the hunger overtaking her. She knew she was gushing all over his face, but he didn't seem to mind. It sounded like it spurred him on because the noises he made got steadily louder without removing his mouth from her pussy. Two more fingers joined the first, and he scissored and curled them up inside her. Stars burst behind her closed lids, and she couldn't even make a sound. It lasted forever, while she clung to the rocks, her mouth open in a silent scream and her body shaking. The moment that she started coming down from the ecstasy, Fern's head disappeared from between her legs.

Not more than a second passed before his hands came to her hips, again. His fingers tightened painfully on them, and he shoved his hard cock inside her in one push all the way to the root. A long deep moan ripped from Iris when he stretched her still pulsing channel to its limits. And then, he started to pound into her like a man possessed. The pain from her skin scraping on the rocks only heightened the pleasure of the thick cock that hit all the way to her uterus.

With each push of his hips, her lower belly bulged, her channel doing its best to accommodate him. Fern twisted his fingers in her hair tilting her head towards his face. When he kissed her hungrily, she tasted herself on his lips, and it drove her insane. Pressing her hands firmer on the rock, she pushed back matching his pace.

Fern became more animal than man. Iris would never forget the noises he made as long as she lived. They were raw, animalistic, and so hot that her wetness now coated not just her thighs, but his as well. New pressure built in her belly.

Fern kept kissing Iris, her whimpers and moans making him crazier with each passing second. Her hot channel kept tightening around his painfully hard cock, and if he didn't cum soon, he thought he might die from it. Then Iris lifted up on the tips of her toes and pushed back harder. His cock sunk deeper inside her and tingles intensified at the base of his spine. He kept pounding into her, her soft ass slapping his lower belly and his sack tightened. Wrapping both his arms around her, one around her waist, one around her chest, Fern lifted her off the ground and held her in the air before he slammed his hips faster. Iris ripped her mouth away from his and screamed his name as her channel tightened and pulsed around his cock so hard that he couldn't keep moving. Fern roared so loud that his ears rang, and darkness covered the brief burst of light. They were both shaking, and he thanked whoever was looking after them that he managed to stay standing and hold Iris up. After what felt like hours but was probably only minutes, Fern came to himself. Still buried inside Iris, he gently lowered her to the ground before leaning his forehead on her back.

"Did we die?" Iris's voice sounded rough.

"No." Fern huffed a laugh, but he didn't have the

strength to do anything more as he struggled to catch his breath.

"Oh, good," she mumbled and went limp in his arms.

Chuckling, Fern pulled out of her, and slowly lowered himself to the ground placing her in his lap. Kissing her forehead, he smiled down at her sleeping face before closing his eyes and leaning the back of his head on the rock. He fell into a light sleep with his lips lifted at the corners.

Chapter Twenty-Five

"Did you find anything useful?" Fern asked Darion when they finally found him wandering through the tunnels.

Iris glanced at Darion's gloomy expression but quickly looked away as blood rushed to her face. The poor guy had to listen to them have sex again. No wonder he was trying not to look at her. She remembered when she had to listen to Artemis and Raphael back in her realm, and guilt ate at her for giving them a hard time. Karma was a bitch, and she hit when you least expect it.

"Nothing but more tunnels. I think maybe Ivy made a mistake. There is nothing in this labyrinth but rocks. Not even another lake like the one we found at the first cavern." Darion avoided looking at Fern too.

"I'm sorry, Darion," Iris mumbled, and finally he looked at her. Fern frowned, oblivious to the awkwardness around him.

"No need, Iris." Sighing Darion rubbed his hands over his face. "It's just difficult to think when you two are very vocal, that's all." Shrugging he gave her a sheepish smile. "I'm starting to think sexual frustration can kill a male."

"What?" Fern's frown deepened as he tried looking at them both without slowing his pace. Iris chuckled at his cluelessness, and Darion grinned shaking his head.

"Nothing, elf. Keep moving. Darion and I understood each other. No need to worry your pretty head." Iris grinned too when Fern turned around and started walking backward eyeing them both in suspicion.

"What am I missing?" His question made Iris laugh.

"Now you understand that him being an ass at the beginning had nothing to do with you, right?" Walking next to her, Darion bumped her gently with his shoulder. "My dear friend is just clueless about most things, living in his own world."

"I have to agree." Iris couldn't help playing along when Fern squinted at her.

"I'll have you know that I'm very perceptive and observant." Fern kept his gaze narrowed at both of them as if daring them to disagree.

"Oh, of course." Blinking up at him Iris did her best to school her features. "Very observant." She nodded enthusiastically. Darion snorted and tried to cover it with a cough.

"Okay, stop. What is this about." Stopping his backward walking, Fern crossed his arms over his chest.

Iris felt terrible to keep teasing him, so she walked up to him, and placed her hands on his crossed arms. His eyes glowing immediately, and she pulled away. It wasn't helping that her stomach did an uncomfortable flip whenever he looked at her like that.

"How would you feel if you were in Darion's place, and he was here with his mate?" The frown didn't leave his face, so Iris pressed her fingers to her forehead massaging it. "If they were doing the things we were doing before we found him," looking up at him she smiled, "and you had to listen to it constantly."

With a sheepish look Fern finally gave Darion an apologetic grimace. "You do have a point. I must be clueless." Darion laughed making Fern chuckle. "I'm sorry my friend, it's just difficult to think when I'm around her. Let's find what we need here so we can get out. I can't promise to not ravish her if it takes longer."

"No need for apologies. I've heard stories about mates although I thought they were bullshit." Indicating with his hand for them to start moving again, Darion continued. "I've heard it's impossible to resist the pull. You two just confirmed it even when Fern was acting bipolar."

"Wha..." Iris burst out laughing, unable to finish her question.

"I told you, you don't even know what that means." Shaking his head Fern chuckled because Iris was still laughing and gasping for air. Darion joined her for a moment, too.

"It doesn't matter. I kind of like calling you that." Shrugging, he shook his head. "I like the word."

They continued through the twisting the tunnels getting deeper and deeper inside the hills. Walking in companionable silence let the tightness of Iris's shoulders relaxed for a bit. She knew it wouldn't last long so she enjoyed it while she could.

Her skin prickled from the unidentifiable energy that saturated the air the deeper they went. She kept her mouth closed not wanting to alarm Fern. His overprotectiveness irked Iris to no end. It was nice to know that he wanted to be protective, but she didn't like it when he thought that included making decisions for her. She knew she was hot-

The First Secret

headed and stubborn. Being honest with herself, she felt a little bad that the poor man didn't know what he had gotten himself into.

"Did you feel that?" Iris stopped moving and held her breath when she felt the ground tremble under her feet.

"Feel what?" Fern was instantly next to her, his fingers wrapped around her upper arm.

"No one is going to steal me away, elf." Jerking her arm away from him in irritation, she glared up at him. "The ground shook. Didn't you feel it?"

"No." Darion and Fern answered together.

"Hmm, maybe I imagined it." Huffing, she stepped forward again. "The closed-in space is starting to get to me. I don't like it." Iris rubbed her hands over her arms hugging herself.

Fern stood for long moments watching her walk away before he followed with a heavy sigh. When he passed Darion, his friend slapped his shoulder as if telling him it would be alright. Fern wasn't so sure. No matter what he did, he seemed to be making a mess with Iris.

"Let me know if you feel it again," Fern said as he caught up to her. "I trust you, Iris." Glancing at her sideways he kept looking straight when she turned to him. "I might act strangely because I don't know what I'm doing. I'm learning how to deal with all the emotions overwhelming me when it comes to you."

"Fern." Looking over her shoulder at Darion, Iris pressed her lips firmly. It's not that she had something to hide, it just made her uncomfortable to talk about feelings when there was someone else apart from Fern listening.

"No, let me say this." Fern stopped whatever she was going to say. "Darion should hear it too because you and your safety mean more to me than my life." Fern also looked back at Darion, and his friend nodded a silent understanding. "I know that I'm overprotective, and I come off as an arrogant brute to you. I don't do it to control you or to prove some dominance over you, little flower. You've been in my realm long enough to see that women are equal to men in every way. Some women are much better at many things then we men are. We honor that, its who we are. But when it comes to you... I'm not even sure how to say this without you biting my head off." Fern chuckled awkwardly giving her a sheepish smile "What I feel... how you make me feel. I want to take you away from everything and everyone. To hide you away so that nothing can harm you in any way. Because if anything happens to you... I will follow you to the pits of hell. There is no life for me without you, Iris. Not anymore."

Iris opened and closed her mouth a few times. Fern's words made her lightheaded and tears prickled her eyes. Never in her life did she think that anyone will love her remotely as much as Fern. His words were so overwhelming that she almost felt sick to her stomach. She wanted to say something but wasn't sure what. Obviously, Fern wasn't finished because he kept talking.

"When things around us happen, like the shadow or even the other Fae being near you. Even just thinking about any danger that might await us wherever we are headed... it makes me crazy. I can't think straight or objectively as I've done my entire life. I act with one thought only, to protect you. So, I act on impulse, and that can be counterproductive. I'm aware of it, so I wanted Darion to know too. No matter what, she needs to be protected." Looking back at Darion, Fern stopped walking. "No matter what is going on around us, or what is happening with me." He stared at Darion intently. "You get my mate to safety."

The First Secret

"You have my word; it is an oath I give freely." Placing his fist over his heart, Darion bowed his head.

Iris felt their power spike as if sealing the words and goosebumps covered her arms. Overwhelmed with happiness, anxiety, fear, and everything else swirling in her chest she walked faster, putting distance between them and herself. Iris needed to clear her head and think, but she couldn't do that with Fern so near. He overtook all her senses, and she totally understood everything he said.

Fern called her name, but that only made her break into a jog in hopes of gaining a little time to process everything he'd said... everything she felt. She heard their thundering footsteps as they began running after her, and like a deer running from a wolf, she bolted through the tunnels. The sounds were getting closer, and Iris knew Fern would catch her soon, but she couldn't get herself to stop. She didn't even pay attention to the ground trembling under her running feet.

One second, she was running on solid rocks, the next the ground under her feet opened like a gaping mouth. For a fleeting moment, Iris felt everything around her stop. Not a sound or even the air moved as she stood suspended in the air. It all came back with a whoosh, and she plummeted into the dark hole.

"FERN!!!" Her scream was swallowed by the never-ending darkness.

Chapter Twenty-Six

Pain made Iris groan as she struggled to flip on her back. She remembered curling her arms around her head. Her magic surged from her chest; bursts of shimmering purple tendrils swirled in the darkness around her. Iris was sure that it saved her life. When her body hit the rocky ground, the pain was so intense that she gratefully passed out. Now, feeling her face pressed in murky water that smelled like piss, she wished she could've stayed oblivious a little longer.

Her hands shook when she placed her palms on the floor and tried to push herself up. Drips of water hitting a puddle somewhere in the background felt like nails in her brain. Her stomach churned at the stench, and she gagged, before emptying her stomach to the side. Iris hoped that Fern would find her soon. She knew that moving far on her own was not an option, but she needed to do something. Another effort to push herself up made her lose consciousness again.

The next time she woke, everything around her was

blurry. Shadows expanded and contracted in front of her. Chills ran up her spine, and cold sweat covered her body before she welcomed the darkness again. The third time, she thought she heard Fern calling her name. Through dry, chapped lips, she called out to him. No words sounded from her throat, only the air from her lungs whispered in the air. The feeling of helplessness overwhelmed her, and she closed her eyes again. It felt like days had passed while Iris floated in and out of consciousness.

Feather light touches gliding on her cheek woke Iris. Afraid to move, so she didn't experience the unbearable pain again she blinked trying to clear her vision. What looked like a spirit, a glowing outline of a humanoid body was leaning over her with one arm floating in front of her face. With her heart thundering in her chest she forced herself to stay still even when everything in her told her to run. Everywhere the hand moved, warmth seeped into Iris's skin. Teeth chattering and breathing in shallow gasps, Iris tracked the movement not daring to startle whatever it was that hovered above her.

"Please." Iris couldn't even hear her own words, her lips barely moving.

The hand of the spirit stopped, and although it didn't have a face, Iris could feel all its attention on her face. Gathering her courage, she took a deep breath and tried again.

"Please, help me." She wasn't sure what she expected, but the spirit tilting its glowing head in curiosity was not it.

Iris barely had time to process what was happening when the spirit lifted off the ground, floating a foot above her where she laid unmoving. Its glow intensified making her squint, while tears blurred everything around her from the brightness. Her breath got stuck in her lungs when the glow moved fast and pushed itself inside her without a sound. Fear clogged her throat, and her body went numb before a bright flash of light forced her to fling her arm over her face. The next second, her body bowed off the floor lifting her up as she gasped.

Panting, Iris spun wildly looking for danger, but there was nothing but rock around her. Her hands throbbed with magic that surged under the surface of her skin, reacting to her panic. The longer she twisted and turned, the easier it became to breathe. When she assured herself that she was alone, her shoulders sagged with relief, and she scrubbed her face with her dirty hands. The stench around her finally registered and her lips twisted in a grimace.

"Oh my god, what the hell was that?" The words rushed out of her and Iris froze.

Slowly she moved her arms lifting them up and touching her face. There was no pain. Stiff and sore, yes, but she wasn't in pain like moments ago. Apart from the horrible smell around her, Iris didn't even feel sick. She wracked her brain, trying to remember all the details but the slipped like sand through her fingers.

"What the fuck did that spirit do to me?" with a horrified whisper, she looked at her palms as if they held all the secrets. "No! I must have bashed my head pretty bad to hallucinate like that."

The plink of drops of water hitting a puddle echoed around her, bringing hazy memories. Scenes flashed in her mind's eye of shadows twisting around her while her unmoving body lay helpless on the ground. Her heart rate picked up, and Iris felt another panic attack coming full force.

"No!" Her voice echoed through the empty tunnels. "It was just a hallucination. I must have a concussion." Pushing herself up, she smoothed her hands over the corset and pants.

Humming gently, she twirled her hand in front of her, and her magic lit up the area around her. The purple glow shimmered and made the dark gray rocks on the walls sparkle. It calmed Iris further, making it easier to center herself and not give in to the panic.

"I need to find Fern. He must be going insane looking for me." Talking to herself eased her irrational fear. She might sound like a crazy person, but better that than to go insane.

Noticing her cloak a few feet away, she went to pick it up. Shaking it a few times, Iris flipped it over her shoulders, lifting her chin in false confidence. It was this cave and the suffocating feeling making her see and hear things, she was sure of it. The longer she thought about it, more convinced she became.

"The elves would never let me hear the end of it if they could see me now." Chuckling softly, she turned in a circle trying to decide which way to go.

Everywhere she looked there were entrances to tunnels. Standing in the center of a round open area it almost felt like she was in a video game where she must pick her next task. A shiver passed up her spine at the thought. Pushing it away, so she doesn't let the panic rise to the surface, Iris lifted her hand and pushed her magic out.

"Which way to Fern?" she whispered. "lead me to him."

The shimmering magic surged and floated towards a tunnel to her right. For the first time after she managed to stand up, Iris felt light and excited. She would find Fern, and everything would be okay. A smile pulled her lips, and her muscles unclenched. Not wanting to wait longer, she rushed to follow the purple tendrils of her power.

Before she entered the tunnel, her magic blinked out and a chuckle made her freeze mid-stride.

"Not that way, child. You need to come and find me first." A deep voice as mesmerizing as it was terrifying floated around her, coming from all sides at once. Taking a deep breath, Iris screamed.

Chapter Twenty-Seven

Looking around wildly, Iris tried to find the person hiding in the shadows. Aware that she was like a sitting duck, standing in the middle of the open space, she sprinted to her right and plastered her back to the rocky walls. Her heart jackhammered in her chest, and her breath came in short puffs.

"Show yourself!" Iris was proud of the confidence in her voice, while she freaked out inside.

"I cannot do that until you find me," the voice admonished. "You need to hurry up now, child, time is wasting."

"Do I look stupid to you?" Her laugh sounded hysterical to her own ears, and Iris cringed at the sound. "I'm not going anywhere until you show yourself."

"You are here to find me. Are you not?" The arrogance in the voice echoing around her pissed her off. "Or have I made a mistake?" A hum sounded as if the person was debating something, and her uneasiness grew. "As for your intelligence...you did drop through the roof, and by the scream, it wasn't intentional. I expected you to find me through the tunnels. I haven't made up my mind yet so I cannot answer your question." Humor laced the statement.

"It was bad luck on my part." Anger spiked in Iris, even though the voice spoke the truth. "I was coming through the tunnels, thank you very much. It's not easy to see in the darkness you've got going here. Which reminds me... Why are you hiding? Surely not because you're scared of little ol' me?" The chuckle that followed caused cold sweat to drop down her spine.

"So much fire..." The words trailed off for a moment. "It's wasted on those you're trying to save."

Power surged through Iris. She didn't know this person but hearing the dismissal of lives she cared about only made her anger and fear spike further. The arrogance in the voice brought back Ivy's theory about her being descended from beings who thought themselves to be gods.

What if she had actually found what they'd come here for? Her thumb moved, touching the tips of her fingers. She should see this through, and if she found that damn secret, maybe they could all get out of these claustrophobic tunnels as soon as Fern found her, or she found him, whichever came first.

"Ah, ah, ah..." Another chuckle echoed, and goosebumps made the hairs on her arms stand on end. "You don't want to waste your power now, child. You cannot harm the one that gave it to you, I assure you."

"How would you know what I'm doing?" Incredulously Iris looked around, still hoping that she'd be able to see where the owner of the voice hid. She found nothing. Only gray walls and tunnel entrances that gaped like mouths greeted her gaze. Not a shadow stirred, or a flicker of movement.

"Hurry up now." The voice sounded fainter. "I've

expended too much energy to announce myself to you. We don't have much time. Too many have invaded this space. I have chosen to help you find what you are looking for, instead of flaying their skin for daring to enter here. Don't make me regret it."

"Where can I find you?" Iris hated the urgency in her voice, but her decision had been made when she remembered Ivy's words. "Which way do I go? Which tunnel?" The questions rushed out of her.

"Ah, that would make it too easy, wouldn't it? Everything you find easy has no value." Another tired chuckle faintly bounced off the walls. "You know the way, Iris." A chill made her skull numb when she heard her name. "Follow your heart. It's the only way you'll find me, blood of my blood." The voice drifted into nothingness.

No matter how many questions she asked, or yelled in the air around her, Iris got no more answers. Whoever the voice belonged to, hadn't been joking about being done talking. At least the fast thumping of her heart on her ribcage had slowed so that she could think clearly.

"Well, more clearly at least," she mumbled to herself as her shoulders sagged.

Blowing a deep breath through pursed lips, Iris rubbed her hands over her face. This was it. She could either follow the instructions and find out if what the voice said was true, or she could act like a scared child and wait for Fern to come to her rescue. She'd never waited on anyone to help her or fix her problems, and Iris wasn't about to start now. The only one she'd ever counted on was herself, so this should be no different. Knowing that Fern would be in less trouble if she did it on her own solidified her decision.

"You are a badass witch, girl!" she told herself firmly, straightening up, and squared her shoulders. "You got this shit down. Let's go find us a secret... unless it's some alien versus predator shit, and then you'll have alien babies popping out through your chest. Oh my god, I need to stop freaking myself out. Don't be stupid, Iris! You got this, you badass, you! You handled Fern's stubborn ass... and Claude. A creepy voice has nothing on you!"

Shaking her arms to loosen up the stiffness in her body, and blowing another breath out, Iris walked with confident steps to the center of the round open space. The faint lighting that gave enough visibility to make her paranoid was pushed to the back of her mind. She would see this through and get the hell out of this place with Fern, and Darion, in tow. The sooner she found it, the faster she would be back to the palace helping Artemis. The pep talk helped bolster her confidence.

Detaching herself from everything, Iris hummed. She'd never questioned how her magic worked or why the need to sing sometimes overwhelmed her. A long time ago she decided to go with the flow, and it had kept her alive this far. The tune that started softly picked up volume fast. Her voice bounced off the walls making the sound more haunting. The skin prickled on her arms and legs, the beauty of it affecting her as well. And then she felt it. A tug from the center of her chest that slowly spread through her entire body, pointing her to the left. When she finally looked around, her focus was on the tunnel furthest from where she stood. Without stopping her humming, her legs carried her in that direction. She paused a foot from its entrance, and the song abruptly cut off.

It was like staring in a black hole. No light emerged, and her feet felt rooted to the ground. Iris had never considered herself a fearful person. She wasn't afraid to walk in the dark, never had the urge for company or to have safety in numbers. That she wanted to turn and run away screaming at the moment spoke volumes about the feeling inside her.

"If only there were something to use as light." Her numb lips barely moved with her murmur, and her hands tingled in answer.

Her brows pulled down slightly as she lifted both hands palm up to look at them. Symbols she's never seen before glowed faintly in the center of her palm. Swirling lines like tiny scribbles pulsed faintly, forming a triangle within a circle. The glow looked like small flames dancing under her skin, but since they didn't burn, Iris didn't question it.

"Maybe I am stupid." Examining the symbols, she laughed weakly at herself. "I never question anything about my magic. What a dumbass." Flicking her gaze from her hands to the tunnel, she straightened her arms, aiming her palms toward the darkness. "Well, no time to start questioning now. Let's hope I'm not the dumb girl in a horror movie that dies first. Here goes nothing."

With a nervous laugh, Iris entered the tunnel.

Chapter Twenty-Eight

Her boots scuffed the tiny rocks sprinkled on the ground when Iris entered the tunnel. Her arms had a slight tremor, and the only sound she could hear was her heart pounding and her blood whooshing in her ears. She prayed silently, only her lips moving. In her mind, she created scenarios where she never came out of the gaping black hole alive, her body lost forever.

Trying to calm herself, and from the fear that clogged her throat, and numbed her body, Iris thought of Fern. When his face appeared in her mind's eye, great calm enveloped her. With it came the realization that she'd refused to acknowledge until this very moment. Fern would be the only person who would mourn her if she didn't return.

Artemis would be sad, they'd become somewhat close in the time they'd known each other, but it'd pass sooner rather than later. Artemis had Raphael, and the stubborn vampire would make sure his mate was okay. Ivy would miss her because her prophecy, or whatever she wanted to call her

The First Secret

visions, would not come true. Darion will miss her as a friend and his hope will be lost about his world being saved. But Fern... he was a different story altogether. Even now, Iris could feel his panic and fear in the center of her chest like it was her own. The symbols on her hip throbbed gently, reminding her of their connection.

Without lifting her feet off the ground, she continued to slide them, pushing pebbles and rocks with her boots. The glow her hands emitted was not enough to put her at ease, so she looked around to see if there was anything else that could light her way. The smell of wet rocks and damp soil insulted her senses. Her fear increased, and she looked over her shoulder to see how far she had come. The entrance was near enough that she could turn around and get out of here if she was smart. Everything in her screamed to turn around and run, but her feet kept moving forward.

"You can do this, Iris!" she told herself firmly, "Don't be a wuss."

Her boot bumped on something hard, and she pointed one hand at her feet, a crease forming on her forehead. A piece of wood lay on the ground half visible, the other half covered in shadow. Crouching, still keeping one hand facing the all-consuming darkness in front of her, Iris wrapped her trembling fingers around the wood and lifted it off the ground. She almost dropped it, the thing weighing more than she expected.

"What the hell..." her whispered words trailed off, and she pulled harder.

Metal jangled, and a slight cracking sound echoed off the rocky walls. When Iris brought it closer, she realized that the wooden handle had a traditional round lantern attached to one end. Another crack made her heart skip a beat before the lantern dropped on the ground with a loud clink, the wood breaking in half.

"Just my fucking luck to break it now, after its been sitting here for who knows how long." Muttering angrily she bent down and lifted it off the floor more carefully this time.

When she had the lantern secure in one hand, Iris straightened up with a death grip on the broken piece of the wooden pole in the other. The tremors in her hands subsided, holding something that she could swing around like a baseball bet gave her false security. She had magic that she could use on anything to protect herself, but this piece of wood was deceptively calming. Flames burst inside the circular glass confines of the lantern, and she almost jumped out of her skin.

"Hurry...not much time..." the voice floated faint and distant from the depths of the tunnel.

Iris shivered and swallowed the lump lodged in her throat. She knew she had to get moving and not lag here a few yards away from the entrance. Steeling her resolve, compensating with anger for what she lacked in courage, Iris set off at a faster pace.

She would find the person who owned that voice, and she'd zap his ass for scaring the hell out of her. She might do it twice because he made her walk in this creepy tunnel, too. Her feet wobbled when she stepped on larger rocks, but with each step, her confidence grew. It's not like she was ever going to back away from this. She'd promised to help, and Iris never backed away from a promise. That's why she didn't give her word often.

Being in the dark unable to see further than a foot in front of her made her appreciate her eyesight a lot more. It made her think of everything that she took for granted as if it was her right to have it and not a blessing to be grateful for. Her feet moved faster; the distraction welcomed. At least she wasn't thinking of dying or what she would find at the end of the tunnel. She breathed a sigh of relief. As she turned the bend in the tunnel, her feet froze in place.

"Oh, my god..." her voice sounded horrified and faint.

Spiderwebs as thick as a curtain covered the tunnel in front of her. They were so thick she couldn't see anything through it. Her hands tightened around the wood. She had a feeling she wasn't far from her destination. Well, she hoped she was anyway. A cold sweat washed over her, but she fought the fear with everything she had. She would not cower.

"You are not human, dumbass. You have magic." Swallowing thickly, she tightened her hold on the broken piece of wood, fingers numb from her tight grip. "It's just a spider. You can stomp on it and kill the bugger."

Gingerly she extended her arm and poked the spiderweb with the sharp uneven end of the broken wood. When she pulled the stick back, the web stuck to it moved with it. Iris almost dropped it. The spiderweb shimmered as a wave of movement pulled on it, and Iris yanked the stick away. The hole she poked in it swayed in an invisible breeze, the stale stifling air around her proving there was no air flow around here. Not one she could feel in any case.

Fern's fear and anxiety battered her chest, and Iris straightened her shoulders. The sooner this was over, the faster she could find Fern. With that thought in mind, she swung the stick, hacking the web blocking her passage.

"I'll be damned if I let you stand in my way." Teeth clenched, she swung left and right until the stick was coated in the spiderweb and she had enough room to keep moving.

Lifting the lantern in front of her again, Iris took one step. And another. And yet another. Goosebumps covered her entire body when she passed the spiderweb, feeling like ghostly fingers touched her soul. Soon she was moving through the tunnel again, only this part didn't look anything like the first part.

A black, oil-like substance coated the rock, making the tunnel wall shine. She felt the sticky goo trying to take hold of her boots as she walked, but Iris had a feeling that she needed to keep moving. If she stopped, she might not be able to get going again. She sped up. She kept swinging the broken stick at every spiderweb she came across. The disturbance in the webs brought their owners crawling out of cracks in the rocks making Iris's heart jackhammer in her chest.

"Stay away from me, you creepy little assholes." Her voice wobbled, and soon she was almost jogging, swinging the stick and dodging webs that stretched from one side to the other.

She tripped a few times over what looked like human skulls, but Iris was so focused on getting the hell out of there she thought her fear might be producing hallucinations. It was getting harder and harder to lift her legs to take each step. The oily substance coating and clinging to her boots made her feet heavy. If Iris was not bordering on hysteria to get away from the spiders that looked as big as her head and were increasing in numbers, she might've stopped to examine it. As things were, she pushed harder.

"Not... Today... Fuckers..." Each panted word was punctuated with a swing of her stick.

Iris could feel their focus on her back burning holes at the back of her head for destroying their webs. The tiny clicking noises of their pincers made an eerie sound that magnified as it bounced off the rocks. Pressure started building inside her chest, and for the first time, Iris welcomed the sensation. Her skin felt like it was on fire making her stumble through spiderwebs that clung to her face and hair, but she kept moving. When the pressure became too much, she didn't stop. A blast of magic burst from her, and a resounding boom made her ears ring. Everything was bathed in shimmering purple for a long-suspended moment. The next, Iris broke out of the tunnel stumbling on the other side.

Whatever she expected to find; this wasn't it.

Chapter Twenty-Nine

Her heart was trying to jump out through her throat, but the absurdity of what she saw made her slowly turn around and gape. It looked like a store ripped straight out of a fairytale. Jars and bottles with suspicious content were stacked neatly in holes made in the rocks surrounding the cavern. Figurines of different shapes and sizes were littered amongst them in varying stages of degeneration, from perfect, to cracked and totally smashed.

Red mist, like dissipating fog, floated around them. It sparkled like glitter, looking both inviting and dangerous at the same time.

"Hello!" Iris called out, wondering if the owner of the voice was here hiding somewhere.

Her voice echoed, and she heard it multiple times coming from the different tunnels sprinkled between the natural shelves on the rocks. Still breathing heavily, her feet moved on their own, leading her to the closest alcove.

A shiver ran down her spine at the pieces of rats and other animals floating in the different colored liquids inside

The First Secret

the jars. Bile rose in her throat and her eyes watered from the stench coming from them. Before she turned away, a small inconspicuous statue caught her eye. Iris sucked a sharp breath in and dropped the broken piece of wood. Her hand reached gingerly toward the figure. It looked exactly like the one she had in her ritual room back home. The one of Artemis. But that was impossible since Iris commissioned that piece from a local artist from her imagination. She has never seen it anywhere else, until now.

Slowly her hand moved between the jars and bottles, careful not to touch anything else. The red mist parted, staying away from her skin and she breathed a sigh of relief. Her stretched fingers barely grazed the statue.

"THAT'S NOT FOR YOU!" the voice boomed. Iris yanked her hand back, and an embarrassing high-pitched scream ripped from her throat.

"Oh, my god, you fucking asshole!" Gasping, Iris pressed a shaking hand to her chest to stop her heart from breaking her ribcage.

Her head whipped around looking for the owner of the voice, but no one was here with her. She felt it in her bones that she was the only living being in the cavern. Holding her hand pressed on her chest, she squeezed the pole with the lantern in her other hand and turned away from the alcove with the statue.

"Okay, Iris. Since that moron scared the shit out of you, it means there is something here that is meant for you. I just have to find it." She moved toward the next alcove closest to her, kicking the broken piece of wood that she dropped earlier.

Iris ignored it, her focus on the items in front of her. More jars and bottles, these were in better condition than the previous ones and thankfully devoid of animal parts, met her gaze. A couple of broken statues no bigger than the palm of her hand lay between them, but she didn't feel the need to touch them. After a few moments, Iris moved on. She walked from one alcove to the next, her heart finally slowing down from its previous painfully fast thumps.

She was almost halfway through the cavern when she spotted a golden goblet. Colorful jewels blinked at her reflecting the sparkle of the red mist swirling around it. Iris looked around first, making sure the asshole didn't decide to show up, before reaching her hand between the jars. She didn't get very far this time either.

"THAT'S NOT FOR YOU!" the voice boomed again, making her jump and stumble back.

Grinding her teeth, Iris stomped forward, looking at the rest of the objects from afar. Ever since she'd fallen through that hole in the rock, she's been spooked enough to last her several lifetimes. She didn't need the asshole scaring her again. Then she saw a necklace that sat inconspicuously all on its own. The red mist didn't swirl around it. It floated close to it just like it did around her skin. Without thinking, Iris walked up to it and traced every detail with her gaze.

A simple metal chain was coiled up on the rock. The copper medallion attached to it had engraved swirls that looked more like some alien language than symbols. The longer she looked at it, the more it resembled a map of constellations pressed into the copper. Fainter lines twisted around them in the shape of human DNA. At the center of it sat a stone that she recognized. It covered the walls of the lake cavern. She'd assumed it was quartz. Now, Iris doubted her guess had been correct.

Forgetting all about the voice, the spiders, and everything else around her, she dropped the lantern not blinking an eye at the loud clatter. Reaching with both hands, her

The First Secret

fingers wrapped around the necklace and she picked it up. A blast of energy passed through her, she gasped, but her fingers only tightened on the medallion.

"That was an intelligent choice." The voice spoke at a reasonable level this time, but Iris ignored it.

"Yeah, a choice," she said dryly not looking away from the medallion. "I'm sure you would've let me know if it wasn't."

"Isn't this what you came here to find in the first place?" Curiosity laced the words, and with a lot of effort, Iris looked away from the medallion in her hands.

Her gaze landed on a well-defined sternum. Iris blinked multiple times, her mind unable to react fast enough. Confused, she lifted her head, tracing the bare torso with defined pecs and shoulders as broad as half of her body was long. Square jaw and thick lips quirked at the corners greeted her. A straight nose and sparkling white eyes with multiple black irises made the breath catch in her throat. Silver hair was tied up in a high ponytail, and few bands were wrapped at equal lengths through it. Arms as thick as tree trunks hung loosely at his sides and golden bands wrapped around his forearms.

"Who are you?" Iris said, barely above a whisper. She gulped, panic rising inside her like a tsunami.

He said a beautiful musical word, but it floated through her mind and disappeared before she could grasp it. The man, or whatever it was, looked at her expectantly. Her neck ached from staring up at him, so Iris took a few steps back to see him better without needing a neck brace for the effort. That made him frown.

"English." Iris dragged the word slowly like he was stupid. "Do you have a name in English?"

"No." Crossing the tree trunk arms over his chest, he watched her with disapproval.

Not wanting to lose the necklace, Iris looped it around her neck and covered the medallion with her hand when it settled between her breasts. She thrust her arm forward toward him.

"Iris." She looked pointedly from her outstretched arm to him before lifting an eyebrow.

"What are you doing?" Still looking unhappy, he watched her like she had sprouted another head.

"Introducing myself, what does it look like I'm doing?" She blinked at him. "Don't they have manners where you come from? Or have you been hanging around with the spiders for too long?"

"You are a strange creature." Tilting his head, he studied her, so Iris dropped her hand.

"Okay…so…" Taking a deep breath, Iris prepared herself mentally for what she was about to say. "I'm here now, and I need to know the first secret." Holding her breath, she stared at him unblinking.

Throwing his head back the asshole laughed, his voice booming all around them. Iris ground her teeth and curled her hands into fists. She needed to get the hell out of here, and she needed to find Fern. Not necessarily in that order. She had no time to waste or a desire to hang out with this guy.

"You think you are worthy, little girl?" The white glow of his eyes intensified while he stared down at her.

"I am of the ancient line! It is my right to know." Iris was freaking out internally and doing her best not to show it. She hoped that she was telling the truth, as this guy could break her in half one handed. 'If I die here, I'm going to haunt you for eternity, Ivy' she screamed inside her head.

"That you are." Nodding twice, he seemed to be debating something.

Iris released the breath she was holding. "I guess Ivy was not full of shit after all. Go figure," she murmured under her breath.

"What?"

"Never mind." She waved a hand at him. "I talk to myself sometimes. So, about this secret?" She placed her hands on her hips hoping she appeared relaxed and not like she was ready to bolt out of there.

"I will give you the secret." His voice sounded excited, and Iris almost smiled. "After you make a sacrifice."

Her lips froze and dread pooled in her stomach.

Chapter Thirty

"Now, wait a minute!" Shaking her head, Iris inched away from him. "No one mentioned anything about a sacrifice. And before you say anything else—" Lifting her hand to stop him when he took a breath and opened his mouth, she looked at him boldly. "I'll be damned if I give anything to you or anyone else just so you can tell me something that I can figure out on my own."

"You will figure it out on your own?" His expression told Iris that he thought her ridiculous. "So many have given their lives for it, but you'll find it yourself?"

"Yes!" she snapped at him, still inching away slowly.

"You are but a child. You need my help if you are to take your birthright. Greater men and women have died in their quest with nothing to show for it."

His words gave her pause. Remembering the story Artemis told her about Lazarus and how he went insane, a shiver shook her body. Her mind spun with everything she knew and all that she didn't. So many things hung in the air, and everyone was counting on her to do the right thing.

The First Secret

"How many of those before me were from the ancient bloodline?" Iris stopped moving away.

He frowned; confusion clear on his face. "None."

"Aha!" Excitement bubbled up inside her, and she gave him a bright smile. "I'll figure it out then. It's not like you were there my whole life teaching me anything. I figured out my magic, and I'll crack this bitch open too. Watch me!"

"You will not break that medallion!" His voice boomed so loud, Iris staggered on her feet.

"Yo! Asshole! It's a figure of speech!" Watching him warily she expected another burst of yelling, but he stood there unmoving. "I'm not breaking anything. I meant I'll figure out how this works. And thanks for pointing out how important the medallion is. I'll start with that."

"You will give your blood for binding, or you will not walk out of here alive, little girl."

"Say what now?" Her anger finally made an appearance, and the medallion pulsed between her breasts amplifying it. "The only thing I give blood to is my tampon. You don't look like a tampon to me. So..."

Iris remembered the time she asked Raphael for blood so he could watch her ritual. The vampire had been smart not to agree, and she wasn't stupid either. Iris had dabbled in blood magic a few times, but the results were always too intense and too binding, so she stayed away from it. If this idiot thought that he would be getting blood from her, he needed to think again.

A sound coming from one of the tunnels got her attention, but she didn't react. It sounded like feet moving fast in their direction, and Iris prayed that Fern had finally found her. She might not be strong enough physically to fight the asshole glaring at her, but Fern could. That would give her enough time to blast him with magic. There was always safety in numbers.

The pounding footsteps grew louder, there was no mistaking it now. Someone was running in their direction, and her thumb moved from the tip of one finger to the next. The pressure started building in her chest. Iris expected the asshole to become alert, or even ready himself to attack. Instead, a wicked smile stretched his full lips, and his gaze twinkled in excitement.

Her breathing speed up as Iris debated if she should yell at the top of her lungs to alert Fern. The only thing stopping her was that she wasn't sure that it was her mate coming down that tunnel. If the sleeping Fae had woken up, it could be some of them. Killing them would only help her, so she didn't want to stand in the way. Iris shifted slightly so she could see the entrance of the tunnel from the corner of her eye while still having a visual on the being standing a few feet from her. His lower body was wrapped around in something that looked more like a shadow than fabric, but she couldn't focus on it too long. Whoever was coming from that tunnel was almost upon them. Her thumb moved faster, and the pressure in her chest reached a level that made dark spots dance in front of her.

"I never said it had to be your blood," the being said softly freezing the blood in her veins a second before a blur of a movement burst from the tunnel.

It took a second for Iris to notice the bare chest and the long black hair floating around the face. He moved too fast. Her magic burst from her, the purple dome of protection missing him by an inch. The shimmering power swirled and circled, but it was too late. Dark tendrils shot from the being close to her, slicing at the moving Fae. One of the tendrils pierced his chest, and he dropped on the ground close to her feet, face down.

"FERN!" her scream was deafening, and Iris threw herself over his prone body.

Tears streamed down her face blurring everything around her, sobs making her body tremble uncontrollably. Iris tried to turn him on his back, so she could at least look at his handsome face. 'Maybe he is still alive' she tried to lie to herself. Pain like she hadn't ever known settled like a boulder on her chest, and she gasped for air between sobs.

"You are crying for one of them?" The asshole now standing over her and Fern looked confused. "They are beneath one such as you. His kind were made so we could replenish our power when needed. Nothing more."

His words stopped the hysteria overtaking Iris. Like a bucket of cold water had been dumped over her, everything stopped. Her sobs disappeared, her body grew still, and all her focus now centered on him. The pain in her chest was still there. But when she stood up and moved away from Fern's body, that too went away. Her fingers started moving again, and a tune she'd never heard before emerged her lips. Everything around Iris faded into the darkness like someone had turned off a light. The only thing she saw clearly was the creature that had taken the only person that mattered away from her.

When moved, the being lost the confusion it displayed. His forehead scrunched up, and a look of shock and trepidation replaced it. He lifted his arms and turned his palm toward her, but the medallion burned brightly between her breasts. The shadow tendrils he sent her way recoiled from her, sinking back into him faster than Iris could blink.

She opened her mouth and spoke the same beautiful musical words that he used to tell her his name, but she didn't understand it. She might not have understood, but the creature in front of her did. He cowered, pure terror on his face before he dropped on his knees and pressing his forehead on the ground. His long silver hair flopped around, and like a rope it curled next to his head.

"I didn't know. Forgive me." His deep voice was muffled as his face pressed to the floor.

"His life was not yours to take! Bring him back!" Iris didn't recognize her own voice. It sounded mesmerizing and like ten of her were talking at the same time.

"I cannot. I am of the shadow, only one of the light can reverse what I have done."

"Well, go find one of the light. If not, you will join my mate."

"I am the last."

Pain sliced at Iris's heart. She was aware that she would not leave this place alive. After losing Fern, she had no desire to live. But first, she would do her best to make this vile creature pay for what he had done.

The ground under her boots disappeared, and she floated upwards, her hair dancing around her face in an invisible breeze. For the first time, Iris heard the magic around her. The shimmering purple that surrounded her entwined with a coppery glow coming from the medallion. Her thumb moved like always, but she finally understood the urge to do that. Her power had a sound, and her fingers moved with the beat of the tune, keeping the tempo of the melody. It was as beautiful as it was terrifying. And in the middle of it all, Iris stood like a conduit. Filtering the life and power from everything around her. She finally understood what she was, but she couldn't find the words to describe it. She was everything, and yet, nothing at all. Just a tiny fragment of something larger than life itself.

The First Secret

That's when Iris saw the blessing. She could save Fern without the creature before her. The question was, should Iris allow him to live after what he'd done? Everything she was in her core screamed to kill him. Because she could kill him if she wanted. Iris knew now that he was merely a lowly guard of another portal. A portal to her real home. But her humanity, the one she had nurtured all her life balked at the idea and stilled her hand. If she killed the being, she would be no better than him. Two wrongs never made a thing right.

Flicking her hand in his direction, Iris sent tendrils of her own magic at him. It sliced his back opening a deep gash and cutting off half of his hair in the process. "Begone!"

He scrambled to his feet, grabbing the cut off piece of his hair and disappeared before she could blink. Slowly, Iris felt her feet touch the ground again, and she turned toward the body of the man she loved.

"Iris!" Fern's voice echoed in her ears, and she clenched her teeth not to cry out. Even now she heard him clearly like he was alive and here with her. "Iris!"

When arms wrapped around her, Iris lashed out sending whoever it was flying into the rocks behind them. Jars and glass bottles fell to the ground, the breaking of glass ripping the silence. Iris froze when Fern lifted himself off the ground, groaning. Her head turned from the body at her feet to the man picking himself off the floor. When his blue, glowing attention focused on her, Iris ran to him with a heart-wrenching sob.

"Oh my god, Fern. You are alive!"

Wrapping her arms around his neck, Iris clung to him for dear life. Fern squeezed her so tight like he was afraid she would disappear again. He was kissing her anywhere his lips could reach while she sobbed and talked incoherently about killing him herself if he scared her like that again. After a long moment, Iris pulled back to look at his face.

"It's Darion, isn't it?"

"Yes." Sadness clouded his features "He said I'd protect you better if he took the first blast. I never expected him to die. I wouldn't have agreed to his crazy plan otherwise."

Iris had a feeling deep to her bones that Darion knew very well what would happen. Unwrapping her arms from Fern, she walked back to Darion's body. Fern didn't need any instructions. He turned his friend to lay him on his back and hung his head in sorrow.

Iris placed her palms on top of the hole that the shadow tendrils left in Darion's chest, and she pulled from the life she felt all around her. Eager to do her bidding, it floated through her and into Darion. Within a few moments, Iris felt his heart thump under her palms. Moving away she set on her haunches and waited until Darion opened his citrine eyes. Fern gave her a heart-melting smile.

"Iris...thank you." There was more relief evident on Darion's face than gratitude.

"You are welcome. And I'm going to kill Ivy when I get my hands on her."

Chapter Thirty-One

"I must say I'm surprised that you're not freaking out," Iris told Fern as she walked in front of him through the tunnel.

"Why would I freak out exactly?" Glancing over her shoulder, she saw his lips twitch, and it irked her.

"I don't know. Maybe because I played necromancer and brought Darion back from the dead?"

Darion grunted something from ahead of her, but Iris couldn't hear the words.

"I knew what I was getting myself into, little flower. You can't do anything that will scare me away. Not anymore at any rate."

"What does that mean?" Unwilling to let him see the uncertainty choking her, Iris continued staring at Darion's back.

"It's too bad that you couldn't see yourself back there." There was awe in Fern's voice, and Iris finally turned toward him. His entire demeanor softened when she faced him. "You floated in the air, Iris. Your power surrounded you, but you looked like you were not present in this realm.

Like a glimpse from a different dimension, a glow mixed with your magic. It was as terrifying as it was beautiful."

"I felt it all, Fern." Swallowing thickly, Iris looked at her feet. "I still feel it."

"Felt what?" He hooked two fingers under her chin forcing her to look at him.

"Life? Death?" Shaking her head, frustration ate at her. "I have no idea. It was so consuming. I know I can take life as easily as I can give it. No one should have that kind of power. No one in their right mind should want to be around someone with that kind of power."

"Why?" The question came from Darion who had stopped as well. "Why wouldn't anyone want to be around you, Iris?"

"Aren't you afraid?" She looked from Darion to Fern. "That I'll lose my shit one day and kill you or something?"

"You won't." Fern smiled gently at her.

"You can't know that." Huffing she hugged herself.

"I will bet my life on that," he assured her.

"As would I," Darion added leaning his back on the wall of the tunnel.

"That's because you're both insane!"

"Iris, look at me." Fern waited until she focused on him and stopped fidgeting. "You could've killed whoever the person was who kneeled in front of you. I saw his power as clearly as I was able to see yours. It was half the brightness that you have. I don't understand your magic, but even I could tell that you were more powerful. And what did you do?"

Hope that maybe Fern would accept the freak show that she was starting warmed her chest, but Iris squished it down. Maybe Fern was still happy about her bringing Darion back, and he didn't know what he was talking about.

The First Secret

"That doesn't prove anything, Fern, and you know it. Lazarus didn't lose his marbles overnight either."

"No, his marbles were never there." Darion laughed making Iris frown at him. His citrine eyes sparkled with so much life that she couldn't stay angry at him.

"You let that man go, Iris. Lazarus would never have done that. Not on day one, not on his last day." Tugging on her arm Fern pulled her to his chest and wrapped his arms around her. "You are just stressed from everything, and you need rest. Let us get back. After you get some sleep and food, we will talk."

Iris allowed him to carry most of her weight and they continued through the tunnel. Darion led the way, navigating expertly from one tunnel to the next. Before she knew it, Iris smelled the breeze of fresh air drifting from ahead of them. Her feet started moving faster, and Fern almost carried her out in his haste to get out of the damn cave.

Iris lifted her face toward the beautiful bright sun when she finally made it outside. It felt like she has been cold for a year while in the tunnels. Spreading her arms wide she smiled when Fern pressed his chest to her back and nuzzled her neck.

"I have forgotten how beautiful you are in the sunlight, little flower." His words were laced with need and Iris shivered in his arms. "It seems as if we spent a lifetime in the darkness down there."

"Tell me about it." Iris laughed, her mood improving with the warmth seeping through her skin.

"I think he just did…" Darion started, but she cut him off.

"Figure of speech!" She squinted at Darion; the brightness painful to her. Darion grinned at her and shrugged unfazed. "How long do we need to stand here before we head back?"

"We are leaving now. Before you argue, I know you can walk, but it'll be faster if I carry you. We will be back safe before you know it that way." Fern looked like he was gearing up for an argument and Iris smiled at him cheekily.

"I have no problem riding you Fern." Hunger radiated from him at her words; she could almost feel it thickening the air around them.

"Let's go. You can hump like rabbits when I don't have to be around the two of you." Darion groaned making Fern and Iris laugh.

Fern yanked her closer and sealed his lips on hers. His tongue pushed past her lips and glided over hers slowly, deliberately. Her knees gave out, and she clung to his shoulders unwilling to break the kiss. Iris moaned softly, and an answering groan vibrated from Fern's chest. Darion cleared his throat very loudly making Fern pull back chuckling. Iris chased his lips boldly, and that made him laugh outright.

"Let's get back so I can ravish you as much as I want." Planting a kiss on the tip of her nose Fern bent his knees and helped her climb on his back.

"Let's move fast please." Iris kissed his neck, and he growled something unintelligible. "Hopefully there will be no shadow thingies on our way back."

"Even if there are, we will be fine," Fern assured her. "You are more powerful than ever, little flower. I can feel your magic from afar. I'm sure they can, too. It'd be stupid to attack you now."

Iris hoped that Fern was right. Both men broke into a distance eating run, and she held tight to Fern's shoulders enjoying the feel of his skin on hers. The scenery blurred around her pulling her into a dreamlike state. Closing her

The First Secret

eyes, Iris buried her face in Fern's neck and breathed him in. His smell of the rainforest and freshly cut grass comforted her, and soon she drifted off into a light sleep. Iris was aware they were still moving, but her mind was on standby. There, but not really there.

When the running slowed down, she lazily looked around and was shocked to see the outline of the palace in the distance. It felt only like an hour or so had passed since they'd left the cave behind.

"Lucky you didn't drop me, I must've fallen asleep," she told Fern making him chuckle.

"I will never drop you. Awake or asleep."

They moved at a slower speed until both Fae slowed down to a walk, way too far from the palace. Iris felt the uneasiness coming through her connection with Fern and stiffened on his back.

"Is it a shadow?" She twisted looking around them.

"No. There is something wrong in the castle." Fern pointed at something she couldn't see.

"How do you know?" Iris tagged on his arms so he would release her. Hopping off his back, she stopped next to him.

"The guards on the top towers are missing. That only happens if we are under siege."

"What the hell? What is this, the middle ages?"

"Maybe our sleeping friends sent a messenger to their group. But that's just guessing at this point. We need to get closer." Fern looked at Darion, and some unspoken conversation passed between them. Darion nodded then bolted left circling around to check the back of the castle, she assumed.

Iris felt strangely calm as they neared the gate of the place she now called home. She hoped whoever had decided to attack was in Artemis's hands right now and that she was teaching them a lesson. Excitement bubbled in her that she could help her friend now. The longer the medallion sat between her breasts, the more control Iris had over her magic.

They glided through the slightly opened front doors, and the familiar smell of the palace filled her lungs. Fern's arm stretched behind him always keeping contact with her body as they silently moved through the hallways. When they reached the enormous stairway, Darion popped his head out from up ahead and shook his head. Apparently, he hadn't seen anyone either. It was a split second between Iris noticing that someone was close by and a hand wrapping around her mouth muffling her scream. Her magic burst out of her, sending the person flying and the thump was loud when the body hit one of the decorated walls.

"Iris, stop!" Artemis hissed from one of the doors to their left.

Looking back, Iris saw Raphael lifting himself off the ground giving her a stink eye. Fern chuckled next to her, and she thumped her hand on his chest to stop him. They all hurried to where Artemis held the door opened for them. As soon as they were all inside a small nicely decorated room that looked like someone's bedroom, Fern stood at the partly open door.

"What's going on?" Iris asked Artemis while they embraced each other.

"I'm just happy that you are alive. I was ready to skin Ivy if you didn't make it." With a stern expression, Artemis looked from Fern to Iris and back. "I see something is new."

"I see you're stalling." Iris pointed out making Artemis grimace as if she smelled something bad. "What's going on?"

"I don't know how, but the portals opened..." Artemis

The First Secret

started, but Iris tuned her out. A voice she'd never forget reached her ears.

"Witch, witch, witch!" Claude's voice filled the silence in the empty castle. "Come out, come out, wherever you are!" he sing-songed, making her blood boil.

"He has Ivy," Raphael spoke for the first time.

Iris's stomach jumped first to her throat, then drop to her feet. Before anyone could react, she ripped the door open pushing past Fern. Rage burned her insides, and she expected to burst into flames at any moment. Iris was done playing a victim. It was time that Claude learned a lesson. Never piss off a witch.

"I'm right here, motherfucker. Come have a bite!" Her voice boomed through the castle just like in the caves while purple tendrils twisted with silver and gray floated around her.

"That's my mate!" Fern said proudly, and he and Darion joined her at the bottom of the stairway.

"Let's go kill the bloodsucker."

When they started up the stairway, they heard Ivy's voice clearly. "This will be so much fun to watch." Her giggle didn't sound like something a hostage will do, but this was Ivy. Anything was possible with her.

Chapter Thirty-Two

On the other side of the hidden portal

"Did you kill the girl?" the voice from the dark figure sounded like rocks grinding together, and the man cowered at his feet.

"No, sir." Clutching his cut off hair, he let the anger build inside him.

"I should have your head!"

"She had help," the man lied. "I was worried they'd find the portal. I did everything to protect us."

"A help that you couldn't deal with? You think me a fool?" His words promised pain and violence.

"The girl is weak. The key will kill her sooner than I can find her. Our plans will come to pass." Lying through his teeth, he pressed his head to the slime on the ground to hide his face.

"Is that so?"

"Yes, sir! I felt her power; she is but a child. I give it a day...three maximum. She will die."

"Good... that is very good." Metal groaned as the person shifted. "You are dismissed. Go keep an eye on things. If you mess up my plans, I will personally skin you alive." After a long pause, the metal groaned again. "If I don't walk out of that portal soon, you'll be wishing for a death that will never come. Being shamed by cut hair will be the lightest punishment."

Not waiting to hear more, the man lifted off the floor and keeping his head down hurried out of the large room. When the massive doors closed behind him with a thud, he leaned his back on it and released a deep sigh. Clenching his fists, he ground his teeth. The stupid bitch almost killed him, but he'd had luck on his side all his life. The first part of his plan had worked. He had a few days to find her and make her submit to him. She was more powerful than anyone he'd ever seen. Including their king who had just threatened him. But he was a smart man. He would bind the bitch to himself, and then force her to destroy them all. After they were all dead, he would be the king and rule over all the realms.

A smile spread over his face, and he pushed off the door. With determined steps, he headed for the portal. Iris would yield when he killed her mate again. She was upset the first time, but if he proved to be stronger, she would see reason. By the time he reached the portal he already had a plan. He would hunt her. And when he found her?

Watching her beg would be so much fun.

More by Maya Daniels

vinci-books.com/devildetails

Heaven wants me dead, Hell wants me on a leash. I just want out.

Hi, I'm Helena and I accidentally opened a portal to Hell. Now, I'm dodging angels, making deals with demons, and trying not to fall for the ridiculously handsome one who claims we're "destined." Spoiler: I'm definitely not buying it. Either way, I'm screwed.

Turn the page for a free preview…

The Devil is in the Details: Prologue
ERIC

When someone you have loathed and been at war with for centuries comes up to you with an offer you can't refuse, you must stop and wonder why. You might think that being cautious and thinking things through so you do the right thing would be more the trait of an angel, rather than a demon, yet here we are. I look at the old man standing in front of me, wringing his hands behind his back, thinking I don't see it. I can smell his righteous disdain for my kind while he is standing here seeking a deal with me.

Nostrils flaring, I let him see my eyes change to their amber hue, and hide my smirk when he gulps, but I'm impressed that he doesn't cower or walk away. He must be desperate. I can work with desperate if it means getting what my father didn't manage to obtain a millennia ago.

"So, let me get this straight," I said, crossing my arms over my chest and glaring down my nose at him. "All you want me to do is kill this girl and the Order, that has been a pain in my ass for centuries, will let us deal with our own

The First Secret

without interference?" Lifting one eyebrow to show how ridiculous I find his offer, I watch him squirm.

"Yes." Clearing his throat, he squares his shoulders and takes a deep breath. "As I said, the details about it are confidential to the Order and do not need to be discussed. All you need to know is that if you kill the girl, we will look the other way unless you or yours get in our way. If that happens, I can't promise that we will let that slide."

"Why?" I ask, and my eyes narrow when I see panic flashing in his eyes.

Catching himself for slipping up and showing emotion, he snarls at me. "Why does it matter to you, demon?" I can't hide the smirk anymore as he continues, "I'm giving you an opportunity no one has ever dared offer and here you are looking a gift horse in the mouth!"

"From where I'm standing, old man, not one of you ever offers anything that doesn't give you the upper hand, least of all to me and mine. So, you'll have to excuse this lowly demon for wanting to know what kind of hole you're trying to have me dig for myself. Now speak! I don't have time for this. I have hunters to hunt and rogues to kill." A menacing smile grows on my face as his eyes widen.

"You don't fool me, Eric! I know a lot more about you than you realize. Take the offer while it's still on the table. I can't promise you it'll still stand if I walk away." Okay, the old man has a backbone, and his words ring true to my ears.

"When?" At his confused face, I laugh. "When do you want the girl dead?"

"So, you'll do it?" There's so much hope in his eyes that uneasiness gnaws in my gut.

Shrugging a shoulder, I say, "What's one more dead hunter to me?"

He squirms again. "Tomorrow! I'll give you the time

and place where she'll be. Just leave the rest of her team alone. But you must do it tomorrow!" His words rush out for fear I'll change my mind. The disquiet grows inside me.

"You do that and she won't be your problem anymore." I listen intently when he mutters the time and place before turning and walking away from him.

"Thank you, Eric. You won't regret it!" he calls after me. My feet falter while my cold heart shrivels. *What the fuck have I just agreed to?*

I almost jog to my car. While driving to see the only person that might make some sense out of all this, my mind reels. The city blurs around me, and before I know it, I'm walking into the reception area of our place of operations. The pretty brunette behind the desk straightens up and starts batting her lashes like a bitch in heat. I might take her up on her offer eventually, but I don't need complications in my life right now. A shiver runs down my spine at the thought of commitment.

"Eric!" she purrs, leaning on the desk and pushing her boobs up. "How wonderful to see you again." I don't come here often. I don't need to be seen to do my job.

"Lauren, is Maddison here?" I give her one of my trademark smiles. Her eyes dilate and her breathing speeds up.

"Yes," she says in a breathy voice while her eyes roam over my chest. I smile to myself. *Silly woman doesn't know what she's asking for.* "She just came in."

"Thanks!" Rapping my knuckles on the desk twice, I stride through the doors towards Maddison's office.

I don't knock. Instead, I push the door open and walk inside where my eyes immediately connect with Maddison's blue ones.

"What's wrong?" Her musical voice usually calms me down, but not today.

She listens intently while I describe meeting the crazy old man. When I'm done, we sit looking at each other for long moments. Lifting her arms, Maddison rubs little circles on her temples. I can relate to that. Ever since I walked away, I've had a raging headache.

"This…" she starts before shaking her head. "This is either the best day of our very long lives, or it's a setup!"

"I'll go with setup."

"Of course, you would." Twisting her mouth in displeasure, she glares at me. I lift both eyebrows. "It's worth the try," she tells me gingerly.

"That's what I'm thinking." Tired, I scrub my hands over my face. "I'll go, and if it's a setup, I'll get my ass out of there as soon as possible. If any of them die in the process, oh, well…oops!"

"You're hoping it's a setup." Maddison laughs, and I grin at her.

"Come on, how bad can it be?"

The next day, while I'm perched on the roof of a run-down house in a shitty suburb of Atlanta, I realize how bad it can be. Five hunters exit an SUV and spread out. The old man said the blonde is my target. What the asshole didn't say was that she'll take my breath away. A fucking hunter and I can't pick my jaw off the roof when she walks over and puts herself between a horde of rogue demons and her team. Her hair floats around her beautiful face with every move. Her breasts bounce, pulling my eyes down like a siren song, and her narrow waist and round hips sway in sync with them. Belts wrap around her lower body and thighs—thighs that I want wrapped around me. Full lips press firmly together, and green eyes flare with the excitement of the hunt and hatred for the rogues. My heart thumps hard against my breastbone when she pulls out two large revolvers, spinning them in her hands before pointing them at the horde. A breathtaking smile brightens her entire face before she speaks.

"Playtime, motherfuckers!" Her sultry voice caresses my ears, and I know that very moment how fucked I am.

"Fucking old man could've just fucking killed me!" I snarl at the starless sky. "I'm fucked!"

The Devil is in the Details: Chapter One

HELENA

One Week Ago

The city passes in a blur as I stare out the window, unseeing, while I replay the last few hours yet again. *'What if's'* have never been my favorite to start with, but I can't help thinking that if we'd done anything differently, then maybe, just maybe, I wouldn't have this gnawing feeling that my life took a nosedive off a cliff and it's headed straight for the jutting rocks at the bottom. *What did I miss?* Questions rattle in my brain, causing my temples to pound with their own heartbeat.

"This should be our last stop before we head back."

George yanks me out of my thoughts when his deep, rusty voice echoes in my ears. I hate the earpieces they make us wear, even though I know how useful they are. Well, useful for the rest of them, anyway; I'm more than capable of taking care of myself. There's no reason for him to use it because we're all sitting in his car, but he likes being a jerk. Glaring at the back of his head, I fight the urge to smack his head on the steering wheel he's clutching in his paw-sized hands like the thing is trying to escape. If you call him out on it, you'll have to listen to lectures of how he makes sure the equipment is working, so the rest of us just grind our teeth and say nothing. There's five of us in the car. Jared, Cass, and Amanda act like it doesn't bother them, but I see their jaws ticking in the occasional light we pass.

Lost in my thoughts, I was enjoying the quiet after our last stop, especially since one of the abominations managed to draw blood before I sent him where he belongs. We are the chosen hunters in North America that protect humans from all things that go bump in the night. Entrusted and blessed by the Archangels themselves—or so we are told—we mostly hunt demons, with an occasional vamp or shifter mixed in. The last stop was a suburb of Atlanta, Georgia, where three demons had nested and had terrorized humans for over a month. Possessing them, they jumped from one body to the next and turned a lovely quiet neighborhood into something from nightmares. Out of nowhere, domestic violence blossomed, neighbors killed each other, and fires and break-ins happened every night. It put a red dot on the area, and we were dispatched to investigate. Needless to say, the demons are no more, and I'll pray that the neighborhood goes back to the idyllic picture the lawns and homes suggested it used to be.

Lifting my arm towards the window, I check to see if the scratch one of the demons left by raking its claws on me has healed. Only thin pink lines are still visible, but those will be gone by the time I take a shower and wash the grime and blood off me. There will be nothing left, not even a scar, but I'll remember the demon's words clearly: *Soon all of you will regret getting involved in things that you know nothing about.* Its raspy voice rattles through my brain.

All of us are blessed with fast healing, longer lifespans, speed, and strength. I would like to think I'm still human, but with each new day after my eighteenth birthday three years ago, I doubt that statement more and more. To make matters worse, I'm even different from the rest of them. My sixth sense is like a GPS for evil, even when the others can't see demons or any of the other evil creatures that plague humanity. It's almost as if evil calls to me, daring me to find it. One thing I've never told anyone is that when that feeling starts inside my chest, it's like I'm about to receive the greatest gift of my life. Excitement and giddiness course through my veins, making me sick to my stomach. It should feel repulsive, yet it doesn't. I've lied to everyone I call friends and family, telling them that it's a sickening feeling because I don't want anyone doubting my loyalties. My conscience is not clear.

"It should be around the corner," George speaks through the earpiece again, making me physically flinch. Instinctively my fist lifts, going straight for the back of his head. Unnerved by the entire night, I'm barely able to control the anger still coursing through me, and he's pushing it. I know, because his dark eyes lock with mine in the rearview mirror every time he does it.

Fast as lightning, Amanda grabs my forearm, and her bright pink nails dig into my flesh. "That's good! We can get it done and go home," she says, emphasizing *home* like she's not glaring at me in the back seat.

Amanda's pink pixie cut hair is styled in teal-tipped spikes on top of her head. Large brown eyes shaded with glittery eyeshadow and sparkly mascara on the long lashes blink from her porcelain face. She looks almost like a doll.

Like those anime characters that she loves so much. We've been best friends ever since I can remember, and no one knows me as well as she does. No wonder she snatched my arm before my fist connected with the back of George's head.

"Yes, I'm actually looking forward to the 'go home' part!" Cass snickers, smacking Jared on the shoulder, making his body twist in the passenger seat to look at her over his shoulder. His blue eyes light up, and he gives her a beaming smile when she grins at him.

"Oh boy! I'm gonna be sick." Amanda groans, rolling her eyes dramatically. "The lovey-dovey googly eyes make me sick." She turns to me again, pretending to gag. My arm slowly lowers, and she stops digging her nails into my flesh, petting my forearm gently before releasing it.

"Yeah." Taking a deep breath, I lean back in my seat and turn to look out the window. "Go in, get out, go home, and no lovey-dovey googly eyes. It works for me."

"Of course, it works for you, Hel! You wouldn't know what googly eyes were if they hit you in the face." Amanda giggles, smacking my thigh with the back of her hand. "Ouch! Move those guns, would you?" She glares at my weapons as if it's their fault she hit her hand on them.

"Leave the girls alone! They're fine just where they are." Petting them affectionately, I glare back at her.

The SUV makes a left turn, and we forget all about the conversation. All the streetlights are broken, and the street is pitch black. Our headlights light up a quarter of it. Bodies with missing parts are haphazardly tossed around like a zombie Apocalypse movie set. My stomach clenches and my entire body coils up, ready to fight as energy rushes through me. Tension rises inside the car as the three of us lean forward from the back seat to see better. This is not something we see every day, even in our line of work. The abominations are getting bolder by the minute, but at least it can't get worse than this.

George flicks on his high beams, and we take a sharp collective intake of breath at the gruesome view revealed in front of us. I was wrong. Crouched above piles of dozens of dead humans are gray, wrinkled demons, their arrow-pointed tails flicking like cats' while they tear the flesh off the bones they clutch in claw-tipped hands. Their heads snap in our direction, revealing red glowing eyes and gaping mouths full of razor-sharp shark teeth. Looking like aliens, with only eyes and a mouth, blood drips down their grotesque faces as they hiss in unison. Everyone else in the car froze, but the anger that I've been fighting all night bubbles like a volcano in my chest. I push the door open and jump out of the car.

"Hel, no!" Amanda's scream pierces the night, but I slam the door in her face.

Pulling both of my revolvers out of their holsters, the usual calm engulfs me like a blanket. Feeling their comforting weight in my hands, I smile at the hissing abominations that turn towards me.

"Playtime, motherfuckers!"

All the abominations spring into action with an eerie screech. Like mice trying to escape a flood, a horde of them bound in my direction. The high beams of the car at my back make it easier to pick them off one by one. The sound of the gunshots energizes me with its beauty. The demons dropped one by one like rocks, their bodies causing those behind to trip and roll on the cracked, uneven concrete of the street.

Shadows move at the corner of my eye as the rest of my team joins me. Blades, throwing stars, and knives fly in the air as they take down more demons. Shouts and hoots sound above my shots as we add more bodies to this street of nightmares, where so many unfortunate innocent humans lost their lives tonight. The pink scars on my forearm throb for no reason, making me hesitate long enough to realize the demons are not trying to fight or defend themselves. They are dying in their attempts to get to me. My team spreads around me like a circle, guarding my back while I'm in shock at the horrifying thought. I almost drop my guns, which makes rage bubble up in my chest. None of them will escape tonight.

That night, the haunting screeching didn't stop until the early hours. It's a night the five of us will remember for as long as we live. I just pray that my team forgets that none of the abominations tried to kill me. Instead, they died trying to capture me alive. Too bad for them. I'm not easy prey.

The Devil is in the Details: Chapter Two

HELENA

Present Day

Scalding hot water pounds my shoulders as I lean my forearms on the tiles and try to wake up properly. The past week has been one intense hunt after another, and they keep getting more difficult. Even with the fast healing, my entire body hurts; the muscles knotted in my back and shoulders feel like tennis balls under my skin.

We've lost so many hunters that it's morbid to walk through the halls of our home thinking, *Say something, it might be the last time you see them.* No one in the sanctuary talks about what is going on, but we all feel the tension building like a ticking bomb with the patrons. The entire Forbearer's ministry has been holed up in the library, only coming out to send us on hunts in groups. The excitement of the chase has gone. No more jokes or slaps on the back while making plans to hang out when we get back. Now, only dull eyes track our movements, like we are going in front of a firing squad. For many, that is precisely the case.

Lifting my face towards the showerhead, I hope the water can wash away the gloomy thoughts clouding my mind. I have the urge to go kick the doors in, storm the library, and demand answers, but after that cursed night, I have secrets to keep. Secrets that might create a bright flashing arrow pointing at my head with the sign 'Imposter' and a reason for me to defend my loyalties. Goosebumps cover my entire body and a cold wave of nausea hits at that thought. My team is the only one not to lose a hunter, and it's not because we're better than the rest. The abominations are more interested in getting to me than trying to stay alive. The four people in my group all keep their mouths closed, even though they watch me from the corners of their eyes. There is a new wariness surrounding us.

Loud pounding on the door sounds over the noise of the water. I turn the shower off, smoothing my hands over my face and hair. The liquid glides down my back, but it's painful instead of soothing. Pulling the screen door open and snatching a towel, I hurry to open the door before whoever it is wakes the entire place up.

"There you are!" Amanda prances inside, pushing past me and acting like she didn't just try to break the door in.

"Are we under attack?" Closing the door, I lean back on it, crossing my hands over my chest.

"No." Grinning, she jumps on my bed, bouncing few times before she settles. Innocently, she blinks her big eyes at me.

"Why are you here at 4 AM?" I'm glaring because this is my time, a time when I can think, collect my thoughts, and not worry about anything or anyone.

"I've been waiting for you to let me know when you're ready to talk because I figured you needed time to process what happened." The mask of playfulness is gone. "Since

The First Secret

you want to play stupid, I figured I'd invite myself in for a heart to heart talk."

"I have nothing to talk about!" Snapping at her, I gather my clothes, snatching them as if it's their fault I'm grumpy, and walk towards the bathroom to dress.

"I beg to differ, and I assure you that neither you nor I are going out that door until we talk." Her voice floats to the bathroom where I drop everything on the floor and lean on the sink with my head hanging down.

She has a point. I know it. She knows it, too. The problem is that I honestly don't know what to tell her. When I look back on that night a week ago, I hope if I ignore it, it will go away." But I must face the music and get to the bottom of it, no matter what it is.

"Did you hear what the abomination that raked my arm said?" My voice is low, but I don't need to lift my head to know that Amanda is standing at the door. Her eyes poke at my back like accusing fingers.

"No," she says softly, as if scared to speak louder in case I stop talking.

"'Soon, all of you will regret getting involved in things that you know nothing about.'" Lifting my head, I lock eyes with her in the mirror. "After that, we lost dozens every night, and each night only our team comes back with the same number as when we left. They don't fight or even try to protect themselves. They're too busy trying to get their hands on me. You can't tell me that you haven't noticed."

"Oh, I've noticed!" She nods adamantly. "But you're a hot piece of ass, so you can't blame them for wanting all those yummy curves!" Her eyebrows go as high as her hairline and the ring she has on the side of her left eyebrow sparkles in the light. She sighs and stops the charade when I just glare at her. "Listen, girl, they're demons! Who knows why they say and do half the things that they do? Our job is not to exchange pleasantries with them. We're there to kill the suckers and send them back to hell. It's what we've been born to do!" Spreading her hands wide, she looks at me as if expecting applause for the speech.

"What if it was right?" Searching her eyes through the mirror, her forehead furrows. Turning around, I lean on the sink. "What if something has changed that we don't know about? I mean, they've never spoken to us." Frowning, I nibble on my lower lip. "Right? They've never spoken before now?"

"Not that I know of, no." Pursing her lips, it looks painful to admit that fact.

"So, my point is," I say, pointing a finger at her, "Why now? And why me?"

"It could've spoken to anyone if it was a Chatty Cathy." Cocking her head, she looks like she is seriously considering her ridiculous statement.

"Amanda, be serious for a second, please. I'm not joking!"

"I know you're not, Hel." Coming closer, she grabs both my hands in hers, squeezing gently. "You are overthinking, as usual. We're the good guys, remember? There's nothing to question or even think twice about." There is so much sincerity in her big eyes that my chest hurts with how much I want to believe everything she says. If only that damn night hadn't happened. "They tell us where the abominations are, we go send them back to hell, and everyone is happy and safe. The good guys always win."

"The good will always win," I repeat, and the pressure in my head and chest lessens. "Thank you! I think it's just the number of deaths this last week that's messing with my

The First Secret

head. It all just hit out of nowhere." Pulling my hands out of hers, I rub them over my face.

"Yeah, I figured it was something like that. You're always the one that takes our losses the hardest. It's not your job to babysit all of us, and you can't save everyone, my fearless, beautiful friend. I just wish you knew what a great person you are and how much we love you for it." Tugging me to her, she wraps her arms around me, squeezing me tight. "Even George, the jerk!" Snickering, she pulls back to look at my glaring face, "I think being a jerk is his way of flirting with you."

I push her away as she laughs in my face while making kissing sounds. Shaking my head, I can't help but laugh with her as I try to place a hand over her mouth to make her stop.

"You're the jerk now! Stop this crap!" Laughing, we wrestle around, and she chortles even louder when I almost lose the towel. The pounding on the door has us both sobering up in a second as I rush to open it, clutching the towel to my chest. George stands at the door and looks me up and down slowly before his dark eyes settle on mine.

"We've been summoned to the library. Another team never made it back." His words feel like punches to my chest as I numbly stare at him.

The Devil is in the Details: Chapter Three

Twenty-five minutes later, I follow my team through the heavy double doors, carved with Holy symbols and intricate crosses, into the library. The musty smell of old books and parchments calms my thundering heart, which is doing its best to push out of my chest and hide as I turn around and pull the doors closed behind me. Reluctantly turning around, my eyes scan everything, marking all corners, shadows, exits, and potential weapons. It's an ingrained reaction I developed in my training through the years, and all my mentors were proud of me for it. At the moment, I'm not so sure they feel the same as three of them narrow their eyes at me when they notice my reaction.

The large room is as big as a public library, but that's where the similarities end. Three walls are lined top to bottom with shelves full of books, one broken by a large window, and a wooden ladder with wheels leans to one side. Between them, a large mahogany desk long enough to accommodate twelve people is nestled with high-back chairs around it. Only four are occupied when we enter, and all the occupants are watching us walk towards them like we're the dirt on their shoe.

My boots make clicking sounds as they touch the fishbone wooden floors and the sound echoes around me as if I'm walking inside a tomb. I don't know why I feel this dread that keeps rising with each breath I take, but my gut feeling has never failed me to this day. I doubt it'll start today, so I know something terrible is about to happen. It even bothers me to know that behind me, when I stop to face those sitting at the table, are rows and rows of books as far as the eyes can see. I feel open and vulnerable. Which is ridiculous, since the sanctuary is an old monstrosity that used to be a church and it's built of blessed soil. It's not a feeling I've experienced often, not that I can remember, anyway.

I'm the last one to stop as we line up shoulder to shoulder and my eyes subconsciously flick to the letter opener that resembles a sword sitting idly on top of the polished desk. That, too, doesn't go unnoticed by the men facing us.

"I'm happy to see you finally decided to grace us with your presence." Samuel, the youngest of the four patrons, glares at each of us in turn. "But I see what the delay was." One of his bushy eyebrows goes up when he settles his mud-brown eyes on me. "Are we all dressed presentable to satisfy your liking, Helena?"

I knew that it would eventually come down to this. For some reason, it bothers the patrons greatly that I'll always style my hair and do my makeup, even before a hunt. Amanda looks like an anime character, and still I bother them more. Apparently, I have too much potential to waste time on unimportant things. They just don't know what's important to me. All four of them now have their eyes on me, and I see Amanda and Cass fidget out of the corner of my eye. No amount of fidgeting can keep my mouth shut, unfortunately.

"I didn't think it would be appropriate to show up here wet and wrapped in a towel, sir! If I knew it was that urgent, I wouldn't have thought twice about it and would've rushed here just as I was when George knocked on my door at 4 AM. I didn't think you would feel comfortable with me standing here half naked," I tell them evenly while doing my best not to smirk when their faces start turning red with each word that comes out of my mouth.

"You should be set on guard duty for showing such disrespect, young lady!" Samuel stutters his floppy cheeks, reminding me of a bulldog. I almost snort at the image.

What the hell is wrong with you! my mind screams at me, but I feel like someone else has taken possession of my body and the words coming out are not my own. Too bad we can't be possessed, so I can't really blame it on that, only on my own stupidity. As I'm arguing in my own head, I see the gloating look that enters Solomon's eyes, and they almost glitter with satisfaction, as if I've given him the reason to keep me from going on a hunt. The dread I was feeling earlier doubles.

"I was told a team didn't return last night. I meant no disrespect, I simply wanted to be ready if we had to leave straight away to search for them." Hurriedly, I try to remedy what my big mouth messed up.

"They were found," Adam says in a hollow voice, cutting off whatever Samuel was about to say.

Silence descends around us, and I look from one patron to the other, waiting to hear more. No one says anything as they stare at us with vacant eyes, not seeing us at all. Absent-mindedly, I glide my right hand over my gun, the cold feel of the metal calming the whirlwind of thoughts that are making me dizzy. Something makes me look at Hector, the last patron in the room, and my heart skips a beat as I notice one side of his mouth quirking before he schools his features. *What's going on? Or have I started hallucinating?*

"Did anything unusual happen this past week on your hunts, or with your assigned tasks?" Samuel continues as if they didn't just tell us five of the people we've known our whole lives are dead.

"Who?" Hearing my own voice makes me flinch internally, and I hear the barely-audible groan from both Amanda and Cass. I want to know which team is lost to us, but I get ignored like I haven't spoken at all.

"There were more demons than usual, sir!" George speaks loud and clear in a voice that would make any drill sergeant proud. "It started a week ago on the day, and it increased daily."

"We all know about the increasing numbers, child." Hector speaks for the first time, his voice deep, fatherly, and even. "We are asking about something unusual, something that's never happened before."

Grab your copy...
vinci-books.com/devildetails

About the Author

Maya Daniels, USA Today Bestselling and multi-award-winning supernatural suspense author, is a fun-loving woman with many talents.

She traveled the world, gaining life experiences that helped her career as an investigative journalist, as well as her storytelling. Maya writes compelling tales of magic, mythical creatures, loyalty, and life-changing friendships with snarky female characters—much like herself.

Her travels have taken her to Europe, Africa, Asia, Australia, and America. Born with her feet in motion, she currently resides in Ohio, spinning her next epic story that you will not want to put down.

Her biggest 'sins' are her love of chocolate and coffee—through an IV drip! One to never sit still, Maya practices Reiki healing, different types of martial arts, reads about the arcane, talks to furry creatures more than humans, picks up a sledgehammer for home improvement, and travels with her fated mate, seeking her own adventures.